AVID

READER

PRESS

ALSO BY LISA TADDEO

Animal

Three Women

GHOST LOVER

STORIES

Lisa Taddeo

Avid Reader Press

New York   London   Toronto   Sydney   New Delhi

AVID READER PRESS
An Imprint of Simon & Schuster, Inc.
1230 Avenue of the Americas
New York, NY 10020

First Avid Reader Press hardcover edition June 2022

AVID READER PRESS and colophon are trademarks of Simon & Schuster, Inc.

For information about special discounts for bulk purchases, please contact Simon & Schuster Special Sales at 1-866-506-1949 or business@simonandschuster.com.

The Simon & Schuster Speakers Bureau can bring authors to your live event. For more information or to book an event contact the Simon & Schuster Speakers Bureau at 1-866-248-3049 or visit our website at www.simonspeakers.com.

Interior design by Erika R. Genova

Manufactured in the United States of America

10 9 8 7 6 5 4 3 2 1

Library of Congress Cataloging-in-Publication Data has been applied for.

ISBN 978-1-9821-2218-8
ISBN 978-1-9821-2223-2 (ebook)

*For all the girls
who've loved before*

CONTENTS

GHOST LOVER

1

THE ONE AND ONLY

YOU'RE IN LINE AT THE HIPSTER SANDWICH PLACE ON A FUNEREAL block in the hills, and you don't want to build your own. You could choose from one of the featured selections, but each is fattening. Pastrami is the polar opposite of Los Angeles.

You had wanted to make something yourself, avocado toast for example, in your gleaming kitchen overlooking the Pacific. But you were out of avocadoes and there was only a quarter stick of butter left, which meant you couldn't yield anything toothsome. You could have had someone bring butter by, but that would have made you feel spoiled and flabby. And even though you would have wanted Kerrygold, you would have probably said *Organic Valley or whatever, just no Land O'Lakes.* And the gofer would have texted no less than twice. *All they have is Breakstone's or Horizon?*

And you would have sat looking at the waves thawing on your

rocky bandage of beach in abject misery, waiting no less than three minutes so that the light-brown-haired girl who was younger and smaller and poorer than you would have had to tarry there, in the refrigerated section, wearing a sleeveless shirt on a gorgeous beach day, for you to reply, *Salted*. Sometimes, the most you could do to make yourself happy was control another being. In the end, of course, it would never work out for you. You would always, for one, be fatter than you wanted to be. Controlling other people adds about five hundred calories. A delicious tropical drink at the bar next to Nobu on the PCH has one hundred more calories, if you're trying to make your assistant pay for the fact that you are on a bad date, by texting her while she is on a good one.

In line you open a bag of Caesar Twice-Baked Croutons. If you only eat half the bag, it will be 170 calories. There is a fly, large and slowed by the greatness of late summer, coasting low. A couple in front of you is playful. Leaning in, the young man inhales the midsection of the girl's hair. She turns to meet his eyes, smiling. They don't hear the fly, which is buzzing loud at ear height. When the lovemaking gaze breaks the boy turns and notices you. At first he barely registers you, because you are not hot and his girlfriend is. And then he recognizes you. He punches his girl in the arm.

—Hey! he says. *Hey!* It's— You're Ari the Ghost Lover! Right?

You feel dizzy, a crouton in your mouth the size of a nightmare. You try to chew it quietly, but there is no quiet, fast way to get rid of a crouton. There is only slow disintegration.

The girlfriend widens her eyes, in apparent recognition. The fly whirs past. Behind you the sooty screen door opens and shuts, and you take the opportunity to turn your head in its direction and chomp the crouton.

—Oh my god, says the girl, it's you!

You turn back to them. Flecks of dried parsley on your lips. She wears a sleeveless Cure shirt without a bra, and side boob slaloms around Robert Smith's ear. Her shoulders are smooth and round. She is twenty-five. You were never twenty-five.

—You're the reason my best friend is getting married to, like, the guy of her dreams! says the girl.

The boy smirks. *Luke* is the guy of her dreams?

The girl punches him and rolls her eyes. They both turn to you.

—No shit, we're going to their wedding in like two months! It's all because of you!

You smile, though you don't mean to. You imagine the girl's best friend is probably a Tier III customer. Although this could have just come from watching your show. It is the only self-help show that has ever been binge-watched, on Netflix. This is something Jennifer, your PR girl, says more often than she says her own name.

—Oh my god, Pandora is going to shit herself when we tell her we met you!

The boy, by now, has lost interest. He is scraping the meat of the girl's waist with his fingernails. Her black jeans are low waisted. Her hip bone is a seatbelt. All he wants to do is fuck her. You are more adept at reading this, you know, than anybody in the whole world.

—You are amazing. You are, like, my hero.

You nod. You resolved a week ago to stop saying thank you. To be icier in general. The decision was made on a day that your sliding door was open to your balcony and a strange bird whined in the distance. The noise of it made you want to pluck its eyes out, and your own. On that day you were the furthest from God you had ever been. You never believed in Him, but on that day you could feel the whole ocean freeze. You felt your toes go bloodless. That was the day the card arrived, sailing forth over the tender shoots.

—Can I— Can we, like, get your autograph, I don't know, or something?

The boy doesn't care, not at all. The fact that the girl cares more about meeting you than she cares about her boyfriend in this moment makes you hate her very much, for having that power. She is lucky. A blind providence afforded her at birth, by how big her eyes were and how tall her cheekbones. At home the screen door is off its track. There is no one you can ask to fix this. There is someone, but you can't ask him to fix it yet. You know it is too soon. That it always will be.

—Next, can I help you! the sandwich guy yells.

It's Sunday, which for you is a whale's throat. Blue-black and forever. People always write and call you on Monday mornings, at 10:27, when you are the busiest. On Sunday, almost never. Not even the old high school friends whose husbands have a rare form of cancer and are looking for a handout. Even those people are too full in their lives to ping you on a Sunday.

The girl and the boy turn to the sandwich guy. Uh, one roast pork banh mi and one TOAO grilled cheese, says the boy.

You remember the first time you came here, and it was with him. He showed you LA like he was opening a sunlit door through his chest. His sandwich place. Scummy but redolent with the smell of half-cooked bread, on a hill over the highway, canopied by trees. The bottles of wine inside, for sale. You could go home with a bottle of wine, and sandwiches.

—No tomatoes on the grilled cheese, the girl whispers, tugging at the boy's soft gray shirt.

—No tomatoes on The One And Only, he says to the sandwich guy, who nods.

—Twenty even, the sandwich guy says. The boy pulls a twenty out of his pocket. It looks like the last twenty on earth, and your heart breaks a little more, when into the boy's shoulder blade the girl whispers, Thank you.

2

THE FUTURE IS FEMALE

On the way to the Country Mart, you dial the temperature down to 60, and draw the flow to the max. Within seconds your face is chilled like a tumbler of milk. You used to worry over how much gasoline the air conditioning was using. Now you don't anymore. When your cheeks are cold, they feel thinner.

It has been almost two years now. In two years you have become something utterly different than you were, at least to the wide world. They didn't know you at all before and now almost everyone does. This is a crazy feeling. Men in Titleist hats and flaccid golf shirts know who you are, because their daughters do. Because your face is all over the place. You are rich. That word! You bought a house in Malibu. On stilts, with one of those driveways, right off the PCH. You used to say, This is not so great. *This* is Malibu? And Nick would say, You have no idea, the other side. And one day he took you to walk along the other side, over the rocks along the breathing water, and you could see the decks and the real fronts of the houses. The fronts were facing the ocean! The *other* side, the *highway* side, that was the back. When you were on the ocean side, you understood how much more these people knew than you, had than you. He held your hand over the sharp rocks. You don't remember wanting more then, but you must have.

Your house is an A-frame. You lied to your best friend about how much it cost, because you felt bad paying for the place in cash when she was struggling across two jobs to pay the nursing school loans off. There is a terrific white bathroom on the topmost floor. A clawfoot bathtub overlooking the water, with golden spigots. Heaven-white towels on teak rods and a bar of soap on the teak stool. Vetiver with French green clay, still wrapped in its furred paper.

You are on your way to the Country Mart right now, for an iced matcha latte and to buy clothes at the sorts of prices that still beguile you. You can spend over two thousand dollars on a sheer blouse, that yet requires something to go underneath it. The less one's body is perfect, the more it needs expensive garments, heavy crepes to position themselves like aid workers across the fault lines.

Still, the old ways cling. The soap in your bathroom is an eighteen-dollar bar. You refuse to use it until you have lost at least five pounds.

The idea for Ghost Lover came, sorely, from Nick. Or rather, from the dissolution of Nick and you. There was an insolvency. The opposite of an impalement. You defecated your soul, is how you marked it at the time, in less refined language, across the pages of your journal. You mourned for months and then you sat in coffee shops and strategized. At first you planned to get him back. There was one coffee shop in particular, on La Cienega, a place untouched by him, someplace he never would have noted. It wasn't precious enough, or clean. There were no whole Arabica beans for sale. There was a fifty-something lady who worked in the kitchen there, and she also came around and tidied up the packets of sugar substitute and hand-swept the milk counter. At first you hated the grunts she made. You hated how shapeless her butt was and how noisy her shoes were. You hated the way she stalked behind you, her toes at your heels like dominos. You were sure that, even though she did not appear to speak English, she was reading the words on your laptop. Your journal entries. Then one day, as she mopped around your chair, she placed her hand on your shoulder. Hallowed, like a mother or a priest. It wholed you. You turned, and her ancient eyes absorbed your depth.

Just like that, everything settled. And you thought, I am fine. I will send him a note. It was his birthday. You wrote, *Happy Birthday.* Sending the words across the avenues of code, you felt like a queen of love. Seven minutes later he replied, *Thx!*

A week later, Nick walked into your coffee shop. With a girl. A definitive girl, about a decade younger. You passed gas, when you saw him. The girl turned in the direction of the sound, and found you. Her face bloomed rose with compassion. He didn't seem to have heard. And she didn't know who you were; she didn't know how once Nick ate you out in your mother's house while Karl, the husband of hers who used to violate you, listened from downstairs.

Importantly, Nick hadn't noticed you, so you ran out, without your computer and your pile of books. You sweated around a corner until they left, in *her* car, which was sporty and black. This made you feel sick. Something about him being in a girl's car. Listening to her young music. When you went back in, the Chinese woman was standing by your table, protecting your stuff with her shadow. She nodded at you. You wanted to cry. You knew you would not come back, would never see her again. These tiny endings are all over the place.

Ghost Lover came easily from there, ideas borne from pain the way moths go to light. You quit your job as the second assistant to a mid-level celebrity. A job you had got only to have a reason to be in LA, with him. You began sleeping during the days, through iced drinks in fraternal sunlight and blondes in bathing suits playing volleyball. You'd go out only at night. Sit in Chez Jay's, which had been his, but you stole it from him. You felt the greasy luxe of being somewhere you shouldn't. The creepiness of lying in wait. You listened. Girls with text messages mainly. How to respond to this one or that one. They didn't know anything. They were young and pointless. But you felt for them, or rather, you felt for the pain in them. Or no. Your pain felt a kinship to their pain, and at the time you had to be wherever your pain was. It was the only thing that was real.

One night there you ran into an old friend of yours from home, pursuing an accelerated MBA in Long Beach and cheating on his girlfriend nearly every weekend. You continued on to drinks at Father's Office. The sweetness of the burger was pink and wrong on your tongue. You sensed he just wanted a place to sleep over in LA. But he was useful, like many ancillary characters; you didn't realize how much, until later. He said the only thing you actually learn in business school is Identify a Problem in the Marketplace and Create a Solution.

That night you ingested over twenty-five hundred calories, at the bar and later at home. You took an Ambien and wrote a business plan until the words melted across the screen. You slept with the friend in business school the next weekend. He felt like a soft iron inside you, something plain and graceless. The dumb pain of simple rod sex. You did not come. He ejaculated largely inside your belly button. The fatty pool of it.

Several weeks later, with this friend's help, you created the application. A forwarding system for text messages so that an expert would respond (or not respond) to a client's crush. The client would be briefed as needed, would otherwise enjoy holy ignorance. A way for girls, mainly, to be the coolest versions of themselves, inoculated in practice against their desire.

At first the expert was only you. You, thinking of how Nick himself would respond to a text. How the young and beautiful girls he was newly with would respond to the texts of grunting men. Quickly, your team grew. You hired small, stunning girls. You always brought on women you would imagine him wanting. One of the reasons was for the angry throb it drew from your pelvis. Another was so that you would never invite him back into your life. You could not feasibly, because there were too many limbs for you to be jealous of. All that superlative hair, all those surfing thighs.

3

BEAUTIFUL WITHOUT LOOKING
LIKE YOU'RE TRYING

There are the girls who please girls, and the girls who please boys. Girls who please girls, even at thirteen, what they do is they blow a boy not to make the boy like them but to go back and report to their girls. The taste and flavor, checking a box. You were in the second group. You always fell hard for boys. Each one was his own fairy tale. One therapist said you got this from observing your mother. Another said it was a by-product of your father's death.

Right now there is one, Jeff. He is a photographer. You have been bringing him to parties. Events that require bow ties. He is always perfumed and ready on time. You-know-who was never ready on time.

You're at the Country Mart to buy a dress for one such event, at the Getty Villa tonight. You come here because you cannot stomach downtown LA. Rodeo, with its chalky sunlight. And the malls are out of the question. You have grown up past the malls. Your tastes have become ultrarefined. You are hopeful today about Morgane Le Fay. You are imagining something breezy and decently transparent.

With this new one you are worried more than usual. Jeff has acquired some gentle fame via you. You suggested him as the photographer for your *Elle* shoot. He didn't want to do the lighting their way, and then he did. Since, he has booked gigs for *Vogue* and *Esquire*. You heard him on the phone with a girl from *W*, negotiating and charming. Jennifer, your publicist, called him *hot* to both your faces. This was vaguely unforgivable, but you forgave it. Privately, to you, and early on enough that she could pretend it never happened, she questioned his motives. You met him on a site for people with more than ten thousand Twitter followers. Either you were hot, or you had a certain amount of Twitter followers. You were in the latter group. He was in the first.

In the store a salesgirl recognizes you. Even in your sunglasses and Bruins hat. You have a pug nose. It is unmistakable. To be recurrently recognized for an element of unattractiveness is a scorching feeling. It makes you want to punish every brown-haired beauty in your path.

Jennifer is the other reason you are doggedly spotted. She is better at her job than anyone else you have ever met. It's mostly accidental. Like all huge successes, she had a few dead-on things happen and now she merely capitalizes on her reputation.

—Are you . . . Wow. It's you.

You don't even nod at her. Sometimes when you eat too much at lunch you need to be cruel to a salesgirl. You finger a flowing cream dress. She offers to start a fitting room for the zero items you have in your hand.

She says a few more things, platitudes both as empty and necessary for you as the hot lemon water you drink every morning, but when she asks if you are looking for anything special, you snap.

—No, in fact. I'm looking for something really un-special. Tell me. What is the *least* special thing you have in the store?

Back outside, you close your eyes against the sun and smush your temples. Oh, the indignity of Sunday!

You open your eyes and send Jennifer a quick text.

I was a mild bitch at Morgane Le Fay.

Montana or Malibu? Customer or salesgirl?

Latters, you write. This is how good you are at your job. You are a clinician of the text. You can eviscerate, palpate, abrogate with a mild word, combined with cunning punctuation. You want Jennifer to have to ask someone what you mean. You want her to feel dumb, undeserving. Like the PR girl that she is. Lest she mistake her thinness for value.

Having bought nothing, you walk back to the car. The sandy mountains in the distance used to confound you. On the one hand, they looked like nature and wild, but then all these boat-shaped villas had wedged themselves into the more hospitable rocks. The houses appeared white and dirty from below, but they were all gated. Nobody used the land they owned. There were horses, but they were dry and hot. The hills of Los Angeles used to confound you, but now you've been to parties in those neglected palaces. You have seen swimming pools used as swan ponds and naked man ponds. You have seen swimming pools that have never been filled with water. When you are inside the mountains, you realize they are not mountains, but placeholders.

You wake up your car and use the key to turn on the AC before you get in. You will wear the red dress that Nick bought you, at that consignment shop in Cambridge. All these years later, all these diets later, you are still mostly the same size. If only people knew how much work went into your weight. The fluctuations in your mind rocket and plunge like an ambitious water slide. Your relationship with your refrigerator has given the cat an anxiety disorder. But on your body the movements are razor bumps.

Anyway, the dress still fits; it's the only one in which you have ever felt effortlessly beautiful.

You will be accepting an award tonight, to become the third annual Golda Meir Ambassador for Women. You have a speech to deliver to a room of very important people. At first you were going to talk about coming from mostly nothing into a lot of something. Nothing anybody hadn't heard before. You were embarrassed by the banality, but you are so starlit right now that it doesn't matter, not even to you.

Then the card arrived. And your bowels released themselves, meltingly, like a spoon of honey submerged in tea.

You took a long, eucalyptic bath. You changed your speech completely.

4

THE OLD PLACE WITH THE NEW GUY

You are meeting Jeff for drinks, before the awards. For his thirty-third birthday last month you bought him a heritage green Triumph, and he loves riding it through the canyons. Lately he has suggested meeting you out, instead of driving with you. You told him you didn't mind the motorcycle, that you weren't scared. But he said that he was, about being a novice and getting you hurt. Anyway, tonight it's a moot point, because of your hair and the wind, and your dress.

The Old Place is another place Nick took you. It was the week you first visited, when you staked your claim. You expressed sadness about the oceans of macadam and the squat buildings. You'd imagined all of Los Angeles was like one or two streets in Beverly Hills, palm lined and arugula grassed. Nick said, Los Angeles is not what anybody thinks it is, before they get here. That's because it doesn't actually exist. You have to make your own LA.

Then he took you to the Old Place in his Subaru. It was terrific. A remote weedy heaven, a warty barn with antlers on the front and horseshoes inside and oil lamps and carved-up wooden tables. It looked like Wyoming and yet there was a Spanish-style villa just around the bend, and a constellation of Teslas. Inside you shared a charcuterie board and counted your quarters. Your waitress, who was beautiful, didn't scare you. You and he were only still friends then. It was a year after college. The Boston years, he used to say, one year on from Boston.

But even then, it was bigger for you. In your journals, there is a red star sticker on the night you met. It was the spring of your junior year and the cops had just busted a party at the Towers. You held a Solo cup in your hand, that you didn't know what to do with.

Nick had met you earlier at the keg. He'd pumped and poured one for you, asking if you liked head. Your eyes widened. On your beer, he said.

As the cops squared their hips at you, he assessed your predicament, ripped off his shirt, and bared his chest to them, like Tarzan. It's easy for beautiful people to disrobe, and cause this sort of a diversion. In any case, you fell for an act of humanity in someone hot.

Jeff, who has become Jeffrey lately in his magazine work, texts that he is leaving now, ten minutes before you are supposed to meet. It will take him forty minutes to come from his studio downtown. He has a drawer at your place, and will sleep over. In the morning he'll go for a run on the beach, and return shirtless. He always leaves a neutral James Perse hanging from the point of a certain rock. He is like an actor in some ways. You'll have showered and applied an invisible amount of makeup and made fresh cashew milk. He'll come in and press his waist to yours and kiss you on the cheek, and you'll want him again. But he always has to go. He is always working, unless there is an event.

It's four when you get there. You choose the same table from nearly a decade ago. A waitress comes by, in her fifties and pock-marked. You order a vodka soda and scan the menu for something with less than a hundred calories. There are no oysters. No ceviche. The better the atmosphere of a bar, especially one in the woods, the more fried the food will be.

You check Jeff's Instagram, because sometimes he will take a picture of somewhere you don't even know he is. His account is a mix of scenic, foggy photographs—glassy bodies of water and tall trees in sunlight—and selfies of you and him, at awards shows and on private jets and in Cannes and in Côte d'Azur. There is one picture that makes you die. You and him at Alexander McQueen, during New York Fashion Week. You are in a purple dress that Jennifer said made you look like a goddess. He is tan and his face is weak but still undeniably handsome. Someone neither of you knew commented, Still Life of Photographer, and a Sausage in Balmain.

You asked him to make his account private that night. Of course, he said. You asked him again in the morning.

Nine years ago you told Nick about Karl at this very table. Karl wore glasses and had slick curly hair, and how your mother loved him.

You told Nick all of it. How you made the fucker pay, literally, for every transgression. Fingered you in the hallway when you were coming out of the shower in your Kensie Girl robe? You used his credit card to buy a pair of Prada sunglasses. Placed your hand over his dick under the table while your mom sat directly across? You bought your gay friend, Bobby, a dinner jacket.

You didn't tell Nick about Karl to get it off your chest. You told him about Karl so that he might love you.

Jeff comes in, helmet in hand. He smiles at the bartender and quizzes the empty room. He sees you, and then he finds you.

—Babe, he says, kissing you across the table.

—Hey, you say, flatly. You have perfected austerity at surprising moments. It keeps people feeling like they have wronged you, and thinking they need to overcompensate.

—You look unbelievable.

—Thanks.

—Are you all set, any nerves I can tend to? Do they have a teleprompter, or are you going off the cuff?

—Off the cuff.

—You are a *beast*.

—I need to tell you about what I'm going to say.

—Give it to me, he says, waggling his finger for the waitress. He is obsequiously polite with waitstaff, yet also urgent.

—It's about my ex.

—Whoa, he says.

—It's about how my ex raped me.

Jeff is the starched breed of new man. He has ridden horses in Texas like a cowboy, but the word *rape* gives him menstrual cramps. He doesn't know the most politically correct way to handle this. Mostly he does not act from his heart.

He gasps. The waitress comes 'round and he is too ruffled to order his drink. He shakes his head. You order it for him.

—He'll have a vodka grapefruit, you say.

—Absolut OK? she says.

—Grey Goose, he whispers. To you, he says, *What do you mean?*

You inhale deeply. It's a complex thing, you say, like all these things are. We were together for a long time. We were very much in love. He was definitely forceful. Arguments we got into. But otherwise, no red flags. He was. I thought he was a good guy.

Jeff nods and shakes his head. Riveted.

You tell him about the night you intend to discuss in your speech. You and Nick were both on mushrooms, but he was unused to psychedelics. He was a beer guy. Your friend Bobby had mailed them to you for your birthday. With Karl's Amex you paid for a bungalow at The Beverly Hills Hotel. You and Nick went out and had drinks at Slumulous with a bunch of his friends because you didn't have your own yet. He didn't want to take the mushrooms, but it was your birthday and you insisted.

Nine years ago, when you told Nick about Karl at this table, he said he was going to kill him. Please, you said, crying. Please, it's over. I just need.

—What? Nick was pissed.

You wanted to say, *I just need* you. Instead you let the pain cramp your features.

Jeff reaches his smooth hand across the table to hold yours. You are steady and alpha and also afraid that you look ugly.

—At some point, in the middle of the night, he climbed on top of me. He was a big guy. Not fat, just. Very broad, and toned and muscular. He got on top of me and sort of, ripped my underwear to the side, like stretched them out. Sorry. Then he started, like, pumping away. Like he was trying to core me.

Oh my god.

I mean, it woke me up. And I knew. I knew he was fucked up. Like, he didn't even know what he was doing. I don't think. It was over before I could even stop it. I don't know how to describe that.

No, I get it.

Of course you do.

Back when, Nick had said, Tell me what the fucker looks like. This was before old people had Facebook. No, you said. I don't know. He's. He looks like someone you wouldn't think was capable. Of doing that.

When Jeff comes inside a condom inside you, you can feel his medium-sized penis begin to contract long before his orgasm has crested. Something tells you this wouldn't happen to him with a hooker. The waitress brings his drink and places it far enough from his hand that he needs to reach, in the middle of you speaking.

—I think it's important, you say, to tell these women tonight. They deserve to know. I think it will help them come forward with their own experiences. Every woman has an experience like this. *At least* one.

Jeff nods expansively.

—I wanted to prepare you; I know that it might be uncomfortable.

—No, Ari. I am here for you. I am here for whatever you need and I just can't believe this happened to you. That you have been living with this. Secret.

The way Nick responded about Karl was wild and bucking. It made you feel like a flamenco dancer, like a woman worthy of killing for.

You sip your drink until it is gone. Jeff orders another because it is all just too much, this information, this evening. The waitress seems to know to bring you the bill. That always happens lately.

5

BECAUSE THE NIGHT

The outdoor theater at the Getty is half-Shakespearean, half-dingy Malibu. Accordingly, you feel tan and legitimate. The vodka soda on an empty stomach was one hair thicker than the perfect amount of inebriation, which is actually even more perfect. You have always been able to alchemize a wrong into a positive. It's one of the ways you got here.

Even the card last week. *Especially* the card. You are about to turn it on its head.

The bar is still being set up and only the important people are here. You, the First Lady, the other speakers, the editors of the major women's magazines, the president of the International Council of Women. Jeff is very good at being unobtrusive. He is not one of those boyfriends who stand in your limelight. He always positions himself just off to the side, so that the glow strikes him well. Cameras always wonder who he is that way; they crane, and he smiles.

—Ari, you look gorgeous! says the editor in chief of *W.* Her dress is spangled and violent. Elvira shoulders, St. Pauli Girl décolletage. Rhinestones in the shape of matadors.

You hate when people say, You *look* beautiful. That is cruel. *Tonight, with that dress and the professional hair and makeup, you nearly pass for one of us. We are proud of you. Welcome, and here is some mesclun.*

You are the second most important person here tonight. You radiate the consummate mix of celebrity and public service required to achieve American glory. You are at the height of your likability. It is minute by minute, of course, but nobody yet wants to tear you down. The denouement will come, yes, but then you can abscond to Greece, Lithuania. You can kill yourself.

But for now, you have arrived. Look at that theater! Soon it will be stocked with broken women in four-hundred-dollar dresses and ten-thousand-dollar jumpsuits. The socioeconomic gamut of coastal American style. You see a woman compensating for acne with a short beige dress. She has nice legs but will never shake the agony of her skin. She is your sister, but you have risen above. You laid in wait, you snake in the grass, planning for this. To be huge. You didn't think it would be about him. You were over it, you said to no one. But you are not. If there had been any doubt that you were still in the undertow, all doubt was expelled Monday morning.

It was classy, of course, because he was elegantly simple and probably the girl is, too. Brown like a bear. Heavy stock. Raised white letters. *Save The Night.*

Not a whole thing, no churches and bearers and limousines. Just a band, drinks, the people they love.

The people we love.

As though you were friends. Yes, you have kept in touch like friends throughout the years. He'd gone back to Boston and you liked him there. He was safe, from blondes in bikinis. From salesgirls in white jeans and baristas in T-strap tank tops. He congratulated you on every milestone, the first time you appeared on Friedkin, and on the cover of *Wired*. Of course he was even more excited to see you on the cover of *Boston* magazine. He texted you a picture of it, magnetized to his fridge. You felt warm in your belly that day, eating only kale and apples.

You saw him as recently as eighteen months ago, when you went home for Karl's funeral. Karl got hit by a car, outside the bar he went to every Thursday with the boys. You were thrilled, but not for the reasons one might think.

For the wake your mother wore her hair in a strangling bun, and the blackest dress you had ever seen. You never told her about Karl. She either knew or she didn't. Anyway, you knew what would happen if the information came from you. You remembered with baleful clarity the trip you took to Destin, just you and her, months after your father died and right before Karl. You were twelve; you hated your hair and had a sickening crush on Douglas Greenway. At the pool of your dated motel your mother lay on a chaise lounge, in an emerald bathing suit and big sunglasses, keeping her body straight and tight in a way you had never seen. You sat at the corner of her chair, blue, but not blocking her sun.

—What is it? she said.

You missed your father but sensed you shouldn't say this. You also missed the boy. He didn't love you, yet. But you felt you deserved something. You knew people so deeply.

—I was just. Missing Douglas.

—Does he even like you? said your mother. You understood she was not looking at you, even though she was wearing sunglasses.

—I don't know, you told her, honestly. He went to the movies with Amber and her mom last week.

You were deaf from the pool water. You'd spent the morning doing leg lifts in the shallow end. Then handstands and hoping your legs looked nice, at twelve. It was three p.m. and you were thinking how long it would take until bedtime, and dreading the darkness at the same time. Florida was all pink clamshells and depression, malls with skylights and surplus palms. Old people, jobless and white. Plus you were in the worst part of it. This motel, this town, not-Miami. A polyp on a turd. The blue of the pool was a cheap blue. It had a urine cast. The sun here was cheap, too.

Your mother inhaled through her nose. She'd been drinking Bloody Marys since noon. This last one had stretched itself into peppery red water. The ice was melted. The celery looked warm.

—I hope you never have a boy, she said, finally. You'll be jealous of his babysitters.

Nick called the day you landed. He wouldn't come to the funeral, but he asked you to Fisherman's Feast. This was right before you'd shot up to intergalactic level, before you'd reached ten thousand followers. You had a nice tan, wore a Cubs hat, and remembered when merely walking through aisles of fried dough with frizzy hair and a boyfriend was enough. He looked dreamy and broad, and cozy like pizzerias in October. And you thought, This could be forever. We could have a child, and Septembers.

—Tripe, yelled a busker. Just got here!

Nick said, Can we get two pounds, rare?

You wrinkled your nose and he ran away. The busker stared at you, presenting a length of tender blond loofah.

You caught up and punched his arm. It was hard and present. You remembered the first time you had cracked him. When it went from him making you laugh to him making sure he had made you laugh. Had Karl helped? Yes. Karl had helped.

Later, walking down Beacon in some bourbon-colored sunshine, you said, Why does Edible Arrangements have a storefront still?

You had been planning all day to ask him if he wanted to get dinner. You felt nervous but optimistic. You had eaten perfectly. One banana. Three snakeskin slices of turkey. But otherwise you hadn't prepared at all.

I think that kind of hope is beautiful, he said.

He stopped walking and looked at you. He asked if you were OK. He meant about Karl. His obsession with how the Karl situation affected you was a Bruce Springsteen song.

—Hey! you said. How about me and you in LA? Do you ever think about those days?

—Oh man, do I. We were fucking toxic.

—But also fucking great, I think.

He laughed, shining his big neck back at the sun, and said, It's crazy, I can't even imagine us, you know, being intimate. I think we were always meant to be the best of friends.

He ruffled your hat. The sky turned black. You utterly lost your shit. Your face overheated. You felt round and faint. There was no way to go back in time, no way to make him unsay that thing which you could never unhear. Your guts were rivering into your bowels. You ran away from him, before you shit yourself. You ran all the way home.

You ate that night with your mother, frozen shepherd's pies, funeral cupcakes brought by women who'd never lost a soul. Karl's empty midcentury chair at the table, everything unheated and ended.

You returned to LA in the morning, three days early. Like always, you regrouped. You ramped up the plan. Purpose bubbled like black fish in your blood.

Become More Beautiful you wrote at the top of the vision board.

But you couldn't do that. So you became everything else.

Karl had left you $250,000. Honestly, it felt worth it. It was a good price. You grew your company by 1.5. You hired Jennifer. The Netflix show came unexpectedly. A wise-voiced man rang you up and offered it, and overnight you became this sensation.

Everything was going swimmingly. There was a plan in place, both heuristic and magical. You were going to lose fifteen pounds, and see Nick again over Christmas. There was a certain amount of success that would make him unable to refuse you. There was a certain weight at which he would think you were pretty.

But then last week, you got the card.

You went to meet her on Facebook. She is Nick's friend Gordon's younger sister. Young and small and honey haired. You had heard that description of hair before, and it seemed trite. But this girl has honey hair. She graduated from Harvard—where you did not get in—just two years ago. You clicked through the available pictures. One of her in a sports bra and eggplant yoga pants. She is a runner. She likes Adidas sneakers and the *Atlantic Monthly*. She likes Jean-Luc Godard and George Eliot and Prince.

Honey hair. Fawn hair. She used the phrase *Damascan rose* in the caption of a picture. She is not funny, but she is not an idiot. One of her brothers is a pilot. Both of her parents are alive.

Because she has a private profile, and because Nick does not have Facebook, you had to be crafty to find pictures of the two of them. You moused through Gordon's girlfriend's account. There was the golden cache. A double date weekend to a tiny house in the woods, one of those hipster getaways. She is in big soft black sweatpants and his sweatshirt. She is in jeans and a plaid shirt. She is roasting a marshmallow in a black knit dress and a tartan afghan. The moon is a bone in the shape of a hole. He is looking at her, in every single picture.

You masturbated to these images, to the concatenation of his newfound happiness and your old happiness, now dashed. Then, needing more, you went on YouPorn, selected category "Romantic," selected sub-category, "Beautiful fucking." There you found a gorgeous honey-haired French girl in a sun-filled farmhouse slicing apples in a plaid shirt. A man comes up behind her.

After you came, you contemplated suicide in the boring, lonely way of unfulfilled, selfish women. But that was last week. You have regrouped (again!). Look at the theater!

Karl used to sweat over you. He was working so hard, he was sweating. The nervousness, it must have been. He kept his shoes on, in case your mom came home and he had to motor. So you would just concentrate on the shoes, pattering against your own naked feet. Deer-colored Bucs. Like a schoolboy. Very clean, never rained upon.

Now you are going to thank the beaten and sexually abused women of the world, really *all* the women of the world, for this award, for your general success, which would not have been possible without them, for your belief in the collective future of womankind, and you are going to tell them what Nick did. It won't be televised, but by the morning all the news outlets will have picked it up. You won't name him, but you will provide enough details that his community can figure it out. Certainly the girl will. You don't think about his mother. You don't think about the things he planted in the ground for you.

Things you won't talk about from that psychedelic night at The Beverly Hills Hotel:

You won't talk about the kissing.

The way your hips rose to meet his on hydraulics.

The way you grabbed his rear harder than you ever had, because you were safe in the pea soup of a drug.

That you *wished* you'd been asleep, that you wished you could sleep through anything to do with him.

That it was the best night of your life. The best sex, with anyone, even with him. Because in the dark you felt loved and wanted, more than you loved or wanted him.

That you were both on drugs, yes, but that nothing he did was forceful. Nothing he ever did was forceful. The only thing that was different was the way he seemed to want you. Like it was the very first time he truly fucking wanted you, as much as or more than he cared about you or felt pity for you or felt friendship for you.

How in the morning you jokingly said, You raped me last night!

How he said, That's not even funny.

—Because you can get arrested?

—No, he'd said. Ari. He said your name like someone who loved you but was not obsessed with you. Like someone who might take care of you forever, if you were open to denial.

—Please, I want to pretend he doesn't exist.

—One day he won't, he'd said.

You ate red and black berries in the sunny patio of the bungalow that morning and read the paper together, but the fear had crept in and was sitting on the wrought-iron bench beside you, your own ghost lover that only you could see. You were always anticipating the day Nick would leave, a pit in your stomach that didn't even keep you feeling full. You knew that he would. So you decided then to leave him first. Would any of these women tonight believe that, of all the things in your life that had happened to you, the death of your father and the sixty-seven times you were palmed or swathed or entered against your will by a man with *tendrils* for hair, leaving Nick was actually the hardest thing you had ever done?

The president of the council introduces you, and you take the stage to TLC's "No Scrubs." In the third row, Jennifer stands in an emerald jumpsuit, her arms folded importantly, as everyone else claps. She has taken up beside an Argentinean model who is dating America's Sexiest Man Alive. Like the rest of them, Jennifer is a starfucker. She thinks people on a screen are more valuable than she is. Maybe you know better, but you are no better. You have learned that the only thing superior to family is people who make money off your success. It makes you reach for the stars. We all need somebody to please.

Jeff claps aggressively on the other side of Jennifer. He is very dapper and his beard looks painted on, from this distance. You feel unmoved at the idea of him, suddenly. Your desire is at absolute zero. Conversely, you always wanted Nick. Even in the effervescing moments right after an orgasm. You always had trouble coming with a man, but never with him. During Karl but before Nick you envisioned your clitoris lying on cement, sped over flickeringly by bicycle wheels. It would regenerate itself and look alive again, but its soul was smashed, bleeding tiny ruby seahorse tears on the sidewalks outside your father's home.

Then Nick made you come through your heart. You didn't need anything else.

All these women will listen, because you have all of their ears. Because you have shown them how to win men, you may now show them how to win themselves. It's time to flip the switch. Paths of celebrity need to be redirected every six months, to keep relevant.

It will be a good thing! Because women will come forward, about their own fingerings and their own *just the tips, just for a minute*, their own predators and assholes and Buc-footed mother's husbands.

Oh, but still, you will let yourself hope. Even after the program this evening, when the nail is in the coffin, so to speak. Like the wrapped soap in the bathroom, you are always saving for a sunny afternoon. Perhaps one day, if the world is emptied by zombies, if all the things that shouldn't matter no longer do, then you will tell him. *I'm sorry. I'm sorry.*

You will cry into his chest. You will forsake the fame, the money, the stilted house, the chilled, silver car.

What devil did you promise your soul? It's no longer a promise. He has it now. He is spinning it into a pink fever, like cotton candy. It's too late. Look at the theater. Look down at your glass-heeled shoes, which are nine hundred dollars. Touch your perfect hair, that smells of nice hotels.

Imagine, if you want, the future. You have enough money that you can envision any development, and deem it possible.

In the future, he will tuck your hair behind your ears, like he used to, his fingers large and full of grace, and say, It's OK.

He will understand; he will understand that these people would not pity you for what your stepfather did. Or they would for a night and then they would think you are gross. They would think about you what you have often thought about yourself. In the shower, when you are scrubbing your thighs. Your stepfather made you lust after soap, made you want to slough the tainted gum of your uterus.

But Nick was a man, a *man*, and real men forgive. Look at your boyfriend there, useless in Armani. It's possible, you see, that Nick was the only good man in America. But it was never going to happen, unless you did these millions of terrible things. You are looking at this rayon rainbow and in your head you are saying this as a mantra. Like a series of locks clicking into place. Like stepping twice inside this square, and skipping these three cracks. Thank God nobody can see inside your head! You clear your throat of pain and useless trepidation and address the auditorium of showered women:

Ladies, you will say. *And gentlemen.*

Los Angeles will be still for you. So will Boston. Your mother, finally, will listen.

It's OK, Nick will whisper, at the other end of this moonless night. *I can take the hit; it will be our little secret.*

Because, he will say, looking at you for the first time like you are a dancer and not a fighter, *because this is how much I love you.*

FORTY-TWO

JOAN HAD TO LOOK BEAUTIFUL.

Tonight there was a wedding in goddamned Brooklyn, farm-to-table animals talking about steel-cut oatmeal as though they invented the steel that cut it. In New York the things you hate are the things you do.

She worked out at least two hours a day. On Mondays and Tuesdays, which are the kindest days for older single women, she worked out as many as four. At six in the morning she ran to her barre class in leg warmers and black Lululemons size 4. The class was a bunch of women squatting on a powder-blue rug. You know the type, until you become one.

———

FORTY-TWO. Somehow it was better than forty-one, because forty-one felt eggless. She had sex one time the forty-first year, and it lopped the steamer tail off her heart. After undressing her, the guy, a hairless NYU professor, looked at her in a way that she knew meant he had recently fucked a student, someone breathy and Macintosh assed, full of Virginia Woolf and hope, and he was upset now at this reedy downgrade. Courageously he regrouped, bent her over, and fucked her anyhow. He tweaked her bony nipples and the most she felt of it was his eyes on the wall in front of her.

The reason the first part of the week is better for older single women is that the latter part is about anticipating Rolling Rocks in loud rooms. Anticipation, Joan knew, was for younger people. And on the weekends starting on Thursday young girls are out in floral Topshop shirts swinging small handbags. They wear cheap riding boots because it doesn't matter. They'll be wanted anyway; they'll be drunkenly nuzzled while Joan tries ordering a gin and tonic from a female bartender who ignores her or a male bartender who looks at her like she's a ten-dollar bill.

But on Mondays and Tuesdays older women rule the city. They drizzle orange wine down their hoarse throats at Barbuto, the dressed-down autumn light coming through the garage windows illuminating their eggplant highlights. They eat charred octopus with new potatoes in lemon and olive oil. They have consistent bounties of seedless grapes in their low-humming fridges.

Up close the skin on Joan's shoulders and cleavage was freckled and a little coarse. For lotion she used Santa Maria Novella, and her subway-tiled bathroom looked like an advertisement for someone who flew to Europe a lot. When her pedicure was older than a week in the winter and five days in the summer, she actually hated herself.

The good thing about Joan was, she wasn't in denial. She didn't want to love charred octopus or be able to afford it. But she did and she could. The only occasional problem was that Joan liked younger guys. Not animalistically young like twenty-two. More like twenty-seven to thirty-four. The word *cougar* is for idiots, but it was nonetheless branded into the flank steak of her triceps.

Now Joan knew the score. For example, she was never one of those older women who is the last female standing at a young person's bar. She didn't eat at places she didn't have a reservation or know the manager. For the last decade she'd been polishing her pride like a gun collection. She no longer winked.

In the evenings she would attend a TRX class or a power yoga class or she would kickbox. Back at home before bed she freestyled a hundred walking lunges around her apartment with a seven-pound weight in each hand. She performed tricep dips off the quiet coast of her teak bed. She wore short black exercise shorts. She looked good in them, especially from far away. Her knees were wrinkled, but her thighs were taut. Or her thighs were taut, but her knees were wrinkled. Daily happiness depended on how that sentence was ordered in her brain.

In a small wooden box at her nightstand she kept a special reserve of six joints meticulously rolled, because the last time she'd slept with someone on the regular he'd been twenty-seven and having good pot at your house means one extra reason for the guy to come over, besides a good mattress and good coffee and great products in a clean bathroom. At home your towels smell like ancient noodles. But at Joan's the rugs are free of hair and dried-up snot. The sink smells like lemon. The maid folds your boxers. Sleeping with an older woman is like having a weekend vacation home.

In addition to the young girls, Joan envied also the women who wake at three a.m. to get stuff done because they can't work when the world knows they're awake. They have, like, six little legs at their knees. She told her therapist as much, and her therapist said, That's nothing to be envious of, but Joan thought she could detect a note of pride in the voice of her therapist, who was married, with three small children.

Tonight there was a wedding and she had to look beautiful. She needed a blowout and a wax and a manicure and a salt scrub and an eyelash tint, which she should have done yesterday but didn't. She needed five hours, but she only had four. She needed cool hairless cheeks. She was horrified by how much she needed in a day, to arrive not hating herself into the evening. She knew it wasn't only her. Everything in Manhattan was about feeding needs. Sure, it had always been like that, but lately it seemed like they took up so much brain estate that a lady hardly had enough time to Instagram a photo of herself feeding each need. Eyelash tinting, for example. Nowadays if you have a one-night stand you can't run into the bathroom in the morning to apply mascara. It's expected that your eyelashes are already black and thick as caterpillars. BE NICE TO YOU, said signs outside Sabon on the way to Organic Avenue. But the problem, Joan knew, was that if you be nice to you, you get fat.

The twenty-seven-year-old caught her plucking a black wiry hair out of her chin, like a fish dislodging a hook from its own face. The bathroom door was ajar and she saw his eyeball out of the corner of her degradation. That was the last time he slept over. He had single-position sex with her two weeks later, but he didn't sleep over and he never texted after that. She remembered with bitter fondness the Dean & DeLuca chicken salad she fixed him for lunch one day, the way he took it to go like someone who fucked more than one woman a week. The more a man didn't want her, the more it made her vagina tingle. It was like a fish that tried to panfry itself.

TWENTY-SEVEN. When Joan was twenty-seven she had started waking with the dry-socket dread, the biological alarm that *brinnggs* off at four a.m. in nice apartments. The tick tick salty tock of eggs hatching and immediately drying upon impact, inside the choking cotton of a Tampax Super Plus. She would wake in an Irishy-weather sweat, feeling lonely and receiving wedding invitations from girls less pretty than her. More than she wanted kids, she wanted to be in love.

But Joan had done better in her career than almost everyone she knew. For example, she had started pulling NFL players out of hats during Fashion Week, when her friends were leaving Orbit wrappers in the back rows of Stella McCartney.

She could have had a man and a career. It wasn't that she chose one over the other. No woman ever chose a career over having a man's prescription pills in her medicine cabinet. But Joan didn't like anyone who liked her. The guys who liked her were mostly smart and not sexy and she really wanted someone sexy. She would even have been OK with chubby and sexy, but the chubby sexy guys were all taken. They were thirty-four and dating twenty-five-year-olds with under-wire bras and smooth foreheads. The problem was Joan's generation thought they could wait longer. The problem was, they were wrong.

THIRTY-FOUR. When she was thirty-four she dated a man who was forty-six, who wore Saks brand shirts and had sunken cheeks and a money clip. They ate at the bars at great restaurants every night, but then she had sex with a gritty LES bartender and she did it without a condom on purpose. Mr. Big, her friends called the forty-six-year-old. They said, What's wrong with James? He's *ahmaayzing*. They said *amazing* in a way that meant they'd never want to ride him. The bartender gave her gonorrhea, which she didn't even know still existed, and it made her feel older than her mother's chewed Nicorette gum, frozen in time and lodged like the miniature porcelain animal figurines, seals and bunnies, that had been left inside the old lady's old Volvo. The same Volvo Joan still kept in the city, because having a car in the city means you can kill yourself gently if you really must. If something awful happens, you have a car, you can get the fuck out.

Tonight there was a wedding and she had to look beautiful because she was in love with the groom. It was the kind of love that made her feel old and hairy. It also made her feel alive.

He was an actor who was thirty-two. She first noticed him across the room at a party because he was wildly tall. He had a grown-up look, but he was also a kid. He was good at drinking beer and playing baseball. That was something she realized now that Mr. Big didn't have, the tufted Bambi plush of youth to make her feel bad. She must like feeling bad somewhat. Everybody did, but she might like it a little more than most.

He was at the bar, so she sauntered over. She walked with her butt light behind her and her boobs pendulous in front of her. She'd learned the walk from a pole-dancing workout class she'd been taking before a superhot twenty-four-year-old brunette with sharp dark bangs started taking the class and even the other women looked like they wanted to fuck her. Why, Joan wondered, were other women her age complicit in appreciating youth?

She ordered a Hendrick's because that was what she ordered when she was trying to get a younger guy to notice her. A grandfather clock of an older woman drinking Hendrick's was a Gatsby sort of thing. It made men feel like Warren Beatty, to drink beside one.

Hendrick's, huh? he said on cue. One thing good about being forty-two was that she had eaten enough golden osetra to be able to predict any party conversation.

Jack had noticed her from across the room also. She was wearing one of those thick crepe red dresses that women her age wore to play in the same league as twentysomething girls in American Apparel skirts.

—Hendrick's, for the long and short of it, she'd said in a husky voice, holding the cool glass up to her bronzed cheek like a pitch-woman. There was something freakishly hot about an older woman who wanted it. He imagined her in doggy style. He knew her thighs would be superthin and also she would be kind of stretched out so fucking her would be a planetary exercise, like he was poking between two long trees into a dark solar system and feeling only wetness and morbid air.

That had been eight months ago. An entire summer passed and summers in Manhattan are the worst, if you're single and in love with someone who isn't. If you're older and single and the younger man you are in love with is not on Facebook, but his even-younger girlfriend is.

Her name was Molly. She had a hundred brothers. Her youth was brutal.

Joan learned about Jack and Molly from Facebook. It made her feel creepy and old to click into Molly's friends and go through each of their pages one by one to see if one of them had a different photo of Jack. Jack wasn't on Facebook, which Joan loved about him.

Thursdays through Saturdays Joan played with the recurrent hair under her chin and moused through Molly's life. She found out in-formation, which is all any woman wants. Some of the information waggled her belly and chopped up her guts into the blunt mince of the sweetbreads she orders at Gramercy Tavern. Like for example Joan found out that a few months prior, when Jack had invited Joan out for an unusual Friday night dinner, it was because Molly had been in Nantucket with some friends. She saw the pictures of furry Aber-crombie blondes and one brown-haired girl on a lobster boat, fresher than a Tulum mist. Joan got superpissed about that. Then she tucked an Ambien down her throat like a child into bed and reminded her-self that they weren't even having an affair.

The most that had ever happened was, they kissed.

The kiss happened at The Spotted Pig, on the secret third floor where Joan was at a famous producer's party and texted Jack to see if he wanted to come by and he brought his friend Luke, who looked at her like he knew what her nipples tasted like.

Joan drank Old Speckled Hen and didn't get drunk and Jack drank whiskey until he became a little more selfish than usual. She was wearing a slip dress and Luke left with some twenty-two-year-old and Jack put his large hand on her silk thigh, and then she took his hand and slipped his thumb under the liquidy lip of the dress and he got a semi and kissed her. His tongue licked the hops off her tongue. She felt like she had eighteen clitorises, and all of them couldn't drive.

One day one month later Jack bit the bullet and decided to pro-pose to Molly. He bought an antique ring that was cheap but looked thoughtful. It was the kind of ring you could get in Florence on the bridge for four hundred euros and pretend it came from Paris. He plans a weekend in Saratoga. He has no idea he is not interesting. He has never wanted for women. Molly's dad has a sailboat they take out on the Cape. At the very least, he will have a summer place to go to all his life. He receives a text the first morning in Saratoga, from Joan.

Hey buddy: book party/clambake out in the Hamptons, couple of directors I can intro. This is a Must come.

Molly was in the shower. They were about to go horseback riding.

He wanted to punch something, or fuck a slutty girl. His anger peed out of him in weird ways. He didn't want to be this greedy about always wanting to be in the right place at the right time. Molly was singing Vampire Weekend in the shower. She had brown hair and makeupless skin. He thought of Joan in a cream satin dress with vermilion lips beckoning to him from a foaming writer's beach.

Joan was staying in a house in Amagansett with a strawberry patch path to the beach. The bedding in her room was vineyard grape themed. What was awful and what gave the whole house a depressed cast was how many times she had changed *shd* to *should*, then finally to *must* in that text. And then capitalized *Must*. She thought of grape must, in her room lotioning her legs, praying to the perfect clouds that Jack would come. She wanted his balls inside her. She wanted him more than her whole life.

BE HAPPY IN EVERY MOMENT, said a sign on whitewashed storebought driftwood in the hallway that connected Joan's bedroom to the bedroom of the fifty-something corporate realtor who was trying to sleep with her all weekend.

An entire forty percent of him had activated plan B. Plan B was, he hightailed it out of the B and B he got on discount from Jetsetter and texted Molly from the road something panicked about something that happened with a surprise for her that evening. They had been dating for six years and she had seen him bring the special bottle of Barolo with him and she was expecting it, so what would be the big deal if he just made up a story about his buddy who was supposed to bring the newly purchased ring to Saratoga, but then the buddy gets tied up at work. It was the best kind of lie, because she would know for sure she only had to wait one more night for a ring. But then a wave of something he imagined to be selflessness washed over him so he wrote back:

Sorry, kiddo. Out in Saratoga, wrong side of the Manhattan summer tracks. You don't know how bummed I am. . . .

In her room sadly smelling the Diptyque candle she bought in case he came, Joan went on Facebook, which she'd promised herself she wouldn't do anymore. She clicked on Molly. She hated when men used ellipses. Why do men use ellipses?

. . . means I don't give that much of a fuck about you . . .

When someone hasn't changed a thing on Facebook in several weeks, then all of a sudden there is a new cover photo of a ring on a finger on a candlelit table, someone else might kill herself. That's something that Facebook can do.

Joan called her therapist on emergency, and she was sitting on the floor of her grape-themed room drinking a glass of red wine in the summer. She told her therapist, I'm on my second glass of wine since I've been talking to you. Her therapist said, We should be wrapping up anyway, but Joan looked at the clock, and it was 8:26 and they had four minutes left, and she wanted to kill everybody. She wanted to kill her therapist's wheaten terrier, who was whining in the background, like he was reminding Joan that other people had amassed a family, while she had eaten at every restaurant rated over a 24 in Zagat.

Molly was twenty-six. It was the perfect age to be engaged for a girl.

Jack, at thirty-two, was the perfect age to settle down. He hadn't rushed like his friends who pulled the trigger at twenty-five for girls whom they were definitely going to cheat on with women like Joan, who you could tell from their lipstick would give wet, pleading blow jobs. Everything with Molly was great. She didn't even nag. Actually, Molly'd asked him when they first moved in if he could vacuum the plank floors, but he hadn't done that yet, so he knew Molly vacuumed, then washed the floors herself. He knew that if her father knew she was cleaning so much he'd be pissed, but he also knew Molly wanted her father to like him, more than she herself needed to like him.

The day of a wedding is always about three people. The groom, the bride, and the person most unrequitedly in love with the groom or the bride.

After fifteen years of not smoking, the day of the wedding Joan starts smoking again. When she was fifteen she started smoking and wearing makeup. At twenty-eight she started removing the makeup, especially from her eyes, with fine linen cloths. At thirty-six she treated each fine linen cloth as a disposable thing, using one for every two days. It made her feel greedy and wealthy and safe. It made her feel old.

Jack is nervous as hell. He is also excited for the attention, even though the wedding party will be small. It is going to be at Vinegar Hill House, a big group dinner after he and Molly sign the papers at City Hall. Molly asked him not to shave because she loves his beard. He thinks of their handwritten vows. He is excited to perform his.

Joan ditches the salt scrub in favor of the eyelash tint. The face is more important than the body if nobody is going to make love to you that night. Without makeup, her face is the color of ricotta. She smokes five cigarettes before nine a.m. and the ricotta turns gray, like it's been sea-salted. By noon she has had seventeen. She has cigarette number twenty and she thinks maybe she should take the car. She's wanted to take the car for maybe seven years now. She keeps putting it off. When Joan was twenty, her father told her she could do anything. He told her not to jump into anything. He told her the world would wait for her.

=======

TWENTY. When Molly was twenty she took a class called Jane Austen and Old Maids. It frankly stuck with her. Today Molly gets ready alone, in the apartment she shares with her husband-to-be. She does her own hair, which is long and brown, and she fixes twigs and berries and marigolds she got from the co-op into a fiery halo at the top. She's naked. The sun comes through the uncleanable windows and lights the garland and she looks like an angel.

She shimmies the ivory eyelet dress on over her pale body. She catches sight of her full breasts in the ornate antique mirror they bought upstate the weekend of the engagement. Coming down her body a tag inside the dress scratches the meat of her left breast. The tag says, *Cornwall 1968*. She bought the dress at a thrift store in Saratoga. Everything that weekend was magic.

=======

SIXTY-EIGHT. Her grandmother and her mother's two sisters died at sixty-eight of complications from breast cancer. Her mother was diagnosed two years ago, at fifty-eight, so back then Molly thought about a decade a lot. Ten years. Now she thinks that it's OK that the past two haven't been perfect. That they have eight left. Her mother is the kind of mother who always had brownies in an oven. Her mother loves her father so much she can't imagine the two of them disconnected, she can't imagine her mother in the ground and her father above it.

She puts on cowboy boots, a simple pair of ruddy Fryes that have been to Montana and Wyoming and Colorado inside horse muck and in salmony streams. The dress is tea length and her calves are lovely. The last time she wore the boots was at a horse ranch weekend with her girlfriends, the month before she met Jack. She made love to one of the cowboys with her boots on in a lightly used hay-smelling barn in the moonlight and he came inside her and Jack never has. The cowboy stroked her hair for an hour after they finished. He said, If you ever decide the big city's not for you, come see me. I'll be here. He had a silly cowboy name and he wore a bolo tie and her friends made endless fun of her. She never felt safer. Now every time she smells hay she thinks of kindness.

Since Molly was seven, she has measured her care for someone by whether or not she would leave snot on their floor. When she was seven and sleeping at her cousin Julie's house, Julie had refused to let Molly have a certain stuffed bear to sleep with, even after Molly cried and begged, even after Julie's mom, who was now dead of breast cancer, had asked Julie to let Molly have the bear, but she didn't *tell* her daughter to do it: she only asked, which was how you created monsters.

Molly cried so much that night that her nose filled with gray storm. In the morning she was less sad than bitter. Tears had dried like snail treads down her cheek and her nose was filled with calcified pain. She cleared each nostril with her child finger and dropped the results, like soft hail, one by one on Julie's bedroom carpet. She left the tissues there, too, hidden under the nightstand.

You could also reverse the test: you could measure how much someone cared for you by whether or not you could imagine them leaving snot on your floor.

Molly walked the three blocks from her apartment to Vinegar Hill House. There was no limo for this bride, no ladies-in-waiting holding her train. She was doing everything herself. When her parents had offered, she'd refused their financial assistance. Her father's money would make her think less of Jack.

When a moment is upon you, the best you can do for it is to imagine it in the past. Like how a whole weekend with friends will come and go and mostly you'll be glad when everyone is gone home and later you'll see a picture of yourselves on a lobster boat in red and blue sweatshirts smiling and blinking against the September suntanless sun and you'll think, I must have been happier that day than I thought I was.

The restaurant is set for the wedding. The mason jars for cocktails, the burlap runners, the long wooden tables, and the bar mop napkins. The wedges of thick toast are out already on rough cutting boards awaiting their marriage to cheese. The votives in Ball jars, the *kombucha* on tap. The ceremony will happen on the terrace, the officiant will be some large-gutted Pakistani friend of the groom's, and it will be shorter than the life-span of a piece of gum.

Her vows are simple and unspecific. She had always thought her wedding vows with the man of her dreams would be specific, about things he did with his cereal, flowers he stole from the grates of Park Slope, picayune habits he had that were annoying, his smelly obsession with roll mops. Jack doesn't vacuum. She was going to work that into her vows and then she felt tired.

For the past two months Molly has been finding tissues. He doesn't vacuum, so she finds the crumpled tissues, like lowbrow snowflakes, in the corners behind their bed, on his side, and also on hers. It is not mere laziness. It is the triumph of his indolence over his love for her, and it is dishonest. She has her dishonesties, too. She asked Jack not to shave because underneath the beard he is gaunt and sallow and looks like the unemployable actor her father promised he would become.

Twenty-six is Molly's perfect age. She thinks of the six years she has spent with Jack, the eight years she imagines she has left with her mother. She thinks of the impending six-minute ceremony, and the forty-three minutes the cowboy fucked her in the hay during which time she came and then came again against the milk-bearded mooing of the cows outside and the whistle of the humble Colorado wind. The ecstasy of grass, the violence of milk. Staring at the wedding bounty before her, feeling the weight of the crown of flowers in her hair, she knows there are hundreds, thousands, who will be jealous, but she doesn't know them by name. She whispers the name of the cowboy to the unlit candles like a church girl, to the naked bread and the tiny daisies in tiny glass jars. She incants the name, and the name itself, like the memory of a moment before it becomes a legend, frees her enough to think the thing she has been thinking for ten thousand seconds, for one hundred billion years, the thing we all think when we finally get what we want. The right way to do something might be the wrong way in the end. Fortunately or unfortunately, both ways lead to Rome.

Joan is on her way, in the car. On her way she receives a text from Jack.

There's a hidden message to you in my speech thing today. Shhh. . . .

Jack is on his way, in a cab. He sends the text to Joan. Not having been employed for a couple of years, he feels good rattling off a text that he knows will go a long way, for his career. It feels like an Excel spreadsheet. Also, how he thought to change *shout-out* to *hidden message*, because it sounded warmer. Finally, on the way to his wedding, he marvels at how easy it is, with women. If only they knew how little time we spend thinking of them, and if only they knew how much we know about how much they think about us. The freaking man-hours a woman puts into men! To looking good for men. The brow tints and whatever. And at the end of the day, you can be twenty-six and it doesn't matter. There's someone out there who's gonna be eighteen, with a smaller vagina. Jack is so happy he isn't a woman, even if he is an actor.

The motor is on in the Volvo in Manhattan and there's a wedding in Brooklyn and Joan reads the ellipsis, finally, for what it is. She reads it all the way through to the end.

At the restaurant with a few Mexican waiters watching her with genuine care and admiration, Molly calls the cowboy's name like he is in the room and like she did in the hay that day and she says it to the wildflower bouquet housed inside the McCann's Irish Oatmeal tin on the wedding cake table. Like Snow White speaking to the forest creatures she leans down and says his name to the ironic bird-and-bee salt-and-pepper shakers, and none of them answer, or come to life. Which makes her feel bummed, but she regroups, because there is a silver lining, like the one in the oatmeal tin that cuts your finger if you aren't careful.

In the distance she sees Jack, though he doesn't see her. She sees him come into the place and check his hair and smooth his beard in his reflection on a dirty window. It's time to do this. Everything is time. You commit yourself to a course in life, to a course of treatment, but nothing lasts forever, not the good or the bad. Molly, feeling the most beautiful she will ever feel, adjusts the marigolds in her hair, and thinks, Forty-two. If she dies at sixty-eight, like all the breast-charred women before her, she'll have just forty-two years left.

BEAUTIFUL
PEOPLE

WHEN SHE HEARD THAT THE BOSNIAN MODEL WITH THE TANGLED hair and the blue eyes died—heroin, Miami—Jane smiled. The model, Petra, had had a thigh gap through which you could see the whole world, Lago di Garda to Prokoško. One less beautiful girl, thought Jane. It was her day off. She'd walked over three miles north, from Orchard Street, on the Lower East Side, through the sixties. The sun was out and also the homeless, who made Jane feel lucky.

On Second Avenue she walked into a cheerless shoe store, and then she headed west, stopping at several small food shops. She bought things that weighed little and could survive her return trip downtown—anchovies wound around puckered capers; a package of white sesame candy. She drank a small bottle of Sanbitter, its color bright red, like fresh blood.

The good news came in a Le Pain Quotidien on Lexington. It was early fall, the temperature of ham sandwiches. She sat outside and ordered a pot of Brussels breakfast tea. On her phone she entered the HGTV Dream Home contest. It was the latest iPhone and she thought of all the things she didn't deserve and all the things she did.

She checked M.B.'s Twitter. *My thoughts and prayers are with Petra's family and friends. Many hearts have been broken.*

She checked her craigslist listing. *iPhone 6 Plus 128 GB, gold. $375.* There was one hit.

How much if you're willing to ship it overnight to Jamaica, NY 11434

She put the phone down. The tea came. Some had leaked out of the pot onto the saucer on its way to her table. The waitress didn't apologize.

Jane needed money, and thought about the Fischl. The painting had come to her the way those things occasionally do. From rich men with bathwater scrotums. It wasn't one of the wild Fischls, the great Fischls. Not the famous Fischl with its splayed lady on the bed and her clockwork of meat and the boy staring at her while he filched money from her purse. Pieces like that sold for close to a million. No, Jane's was called *The Welcome.* In the foreground, on a beach, propped on one elbow, is a middle-aged woman, sunbathing nude, her bare backside facing the viewer, her G-string tan lines bright against her sunburn, her brown hair in two loose, sensual, slightly age-inappropriate pigtails. She is greeting a mostly bald middle-aged man walking toward her along the water's edge. He is broad shouldered, with powerful arms; he has nice pecs but a slight gut; he wears stylish black shorts. Everyone in the background is also middle-aged, with medium-rare bellies. One man wears goggles; another has a towel draped around his neck, as if he's cold. The woman's back is flabby but tan and inviting; there is something unabashed about her. The sand is hard. The ocean looks rich. Everybody in the picture drinks good wine in early evenings, Jane thought. Good, white wine.

She could easily sell it for forty grand, but had never given it serious thought. If she sold it, that would be the end.

She thumbed through the dead model's Instagram again.

Petra in a wet white dress on a Caribbean beach, holding a teddy bear holding a heart that says, *Shit bitch you is fine*.

In Fryes and panties and a leather jacket sitting on the hood of a Jeep Wrangler, smoking a cigarette. Tiny, tanned legs parted. Four hundred twenty-two comments.

In the desert, wearing a flannel shirt, scrunched-up face, matted hair, holding a Pabst and flipping the horizon the bird.

In cornrows, thumbs-upping a plate of Mexican food.

At Halloween, as Martha Kelly from *Baskets*. Jane marveled at the club of beautiful women, who wore granny dresses or horrific makeup on Halloween as though to say, *I am beautiful every day of the year, but tonight I will hide, so you may shine.*

Next a selfie. In a hotel bed, smiling sideways. Hotel stationery on the other pillow, folded and positioned so you could only read the salutation. *Dear Petra.* There was a daisy beside the note. Caption: *My secret friend . . .*

Jane saw that one last week. She'd been triangulating Petra's feed for months. It wasn't serious; the model was too dumb for him, too much of a druggie. And yet there was more to their relationship than just fucking. She was a night crawler. Seedy and beautiful. She wasn't classy enough for a place like San Sebastián, but wherever that hotel was, with the daisy, he took her there. Maybe London. London was seedy and beautiful, too.

When Jane switched to his Instagram feed, she gasped.

It was a photograph of *The Welcome*. Before it belonged to the man who gave it to Jane, it was in a SoHo gallery, and the dead model had snapped a picture of herself—younger but not necessarily hotter—in front of it. Or he had.

#tbt, said the caption, *to when life was simpler . . . I wanna be this chic, you said. She has the Secret.*

Jane had never gasped a day in her life, not even on the one when she received the phone call—father, pistol, end. She made the image bigger with her fingers. She studied the corners. Absently she felt for a pimple that had been growing on her shoulder blade.

═══════════

The next day, Jane walked west, wearing new flats and a pale-yellow sundress. It was juicy hot, but the bodega men were still selling buttered rolls and the butter melted into liquid that filled every nook and cranny of the bread.

The movie set was on Bedford Street, a brownstone with a quaint patio, a shale and ivy little prison. The West Village was standing in for Prospect Heights. The other day they'd shot a garden party scene, on the patio, wherein the husband and the wife entertained the parents of their young daughter's friend. Pinot Grigio and fingerlings. The two child actresses, ten and eleven, tongue-kissed for a selfie as it started to rain.

This morning was a breakfast scene, and it was just him. Him and Jane and seventeen other people who could have died, who should have died. If they died, then it would just be him and her and taxis and homeless men and he would have no choice.

On Bedford she approached the prop truck, a Mercedes Sprinter van. She gave Ricky the driver the go-ahead to start unloading. He'd been sitting on the curb, vaping. A carabiner around the belt loop of his saggy jeans held all the keys. His eyes looked raw and she hated to be alone with him, even on a city street.

—I need just, uh, the Section C stuff, Jane said. She was better at telling men what to do than women.

Ricky nodded and winked a yellow eye. Jane knew some of the men only wanted to fuck her when she was in their faces, while others thought about it multiple times a day. On this set, she also understood she was the only thing going. The female crew members were old and Patagonia, or older and chemical peeled. There were two hot actresses on the film—one blonde, one redhead—who raised everyone's temperature, but guys like Ricky, guys like the dolly grip and the DP and all the other freaks and losers, knew they had no chance. They smelled like beer and ate enchiladas and talked about old arcade games and fetish porn. They didn't even fantasize about the actresses. During breakdown, as the sun cooled and Manhattan twinkled with possibility—rape and cocktails and OpenTable—the men swiped on Tinder and looked at Jane and texted things like, *What u up to after.* She could see them across the living room of the brownstone, their phones in thick OtterBox cases, held keenly below their guts.

———

Jane walked past craft service—pineapples in white plastic bowls, triangles of cheddar, too many plum tomatoes. Up the plasma steps, into the slim, brick Greek Revival town home. Jane hated the owners, an artist couple with fantastic taste whom she had not met. The wife's parents had bought them a seven-million-dollar place on a great block. The husband used triple-crème cheeses in the kids' omelettes and the wife intimated it was all thanks to his lithographs. Both wrote plays.

The interior was appropriately condomed, with black mats on the wood-plank floor and corrugated cardboard against the walls. The Japanese tea-ceremony table, nearly the length of the room, was covered with a blue sound blanket. All the other furniture was Bubble

Wrapped and clustered in the corners. Jane always thought a film crew would make sensible murderers.

The only indoor shot they were filming today was of the slate breakfast nook, where M.B., playing Ben Coates, would make himself a SuperGreens smoothie and carry it outside. As prop master, Jane was in charge of swapping out the owners' Vitamix for the one she'd bought last week.

Noticed you have a Vitamix, Jane had emailed the wife a week before filming began—*would be great if we could use it, just one shot, for greens and maybe some blueberries.*

Yikes, the wife wrote back thirty-six hours later, *Seb & Noodle are allergic to most vine fruits. Even when something is washed out, it can leave a residue. Can't risk it. . . . Sorry!*

Jane was also responsible for M.B.'s clothes for the day, a pair of rust-colored khakis and a white T-shirt. The costume designer, Nicole, had tried to relieve her of the task.

—I can handle the clothes, since they're mine, said Nicole on the first day of filming. In fact, she added, winking, it would be my pleasure.

—Yeah, said Jane, thanks. But they're my responsibility to bring and to maintain, and I can't risk it. Sorry.

Jane slept in the white T-shirt last night. She showered and put it on over her damp skin. No panties. Got into bed and rubbed her breasts over the material and touched herself. It was a Large, so she could just tuck it, like a diaper, between her thighs.

———

By ten the more important people had arrived. Trib, the director—headphones, muttonchops—was in the video village sipping a matcha latte. He rode a Citi Bike to work from the Greenwich Hotel, where M.B. was also staying and where even the rain was more beautiful.

Jane was at the outdoor table. The AD, a crabby divorcée, handed her a plastic tub of Organic Girl supergreens and told her to remove the leaves that had gone bad. They could have had an intern get a new container for $3.99, but movie sets were parsimonious with certain things. So Jane sat there, peeling dark-green wet leaves of tatsoi from dry ones. Chlorophyll collected under her nails.

Lyle Lovett's "Private Conversation" was playing from the speaker. She had twenty minutes to fix herself in the bathroom before he arrived. When she was nervous her pores released more oil, so she took a break from the leaves and pulled blotting papers from her jeans pocket. She tapped her foot to the beat, pressed the paper to the side of her nose, and looked at it: transparent with grease. She heard a sound and turned.

This was God. This was life. Fucking and unfucking you with the chanciness of cancer.

He was early.

———

There are wolves and there are foxes and there are ptarmigans and there are agents and there are women you can pay to kick you in the balls with the sharp patent toe of a shoe you bought them for that express purpose. There are politicians who are famous. There are famous actors and then there are men who are not only beautiful and charming but are born with something extra. The close-togetherness of pashmina; green eyes that can actually finger you.

—Jane, he said, like he knew she would be happy to hear him say her name.

She shot up, folded the blotting paper in two, and snapped it into her fist.

—Hey!

He smiled and sat down at the teak table with a *venti* cup. The sun was what the sun can be when the sun is only for you.

He leaned back in the chair and thrust his knees forward. He clasped his hands. He was elite and she was a Budget truck. She was a shitty painting a housewife does over Chablis in suburban New Jersey. Fuzzy trees and a cartoon moon. Hang it in the second kid's nursery and fucking kill yourself.

—Do you want some coffee? he asked. I'll go get us mugs.

She figured he would never come back. But he did, with two camp mugs the color of a planetarium sky. He poured black coffee into both and passed one to Jane.

—I'm sorry about Petra; I heard you guys were friends. Jane was good at saying things others were too Anglican to say.

—Hey, thanks. Yeah. We were close. I'm still in shock.

He looked down. She thought of the dead model kneeling between his legs. She wondered if, when two people with interstellar looks fucked, it was blander somehow. Like Barbie and Ken, smooth plastic bumping, minimal juices, clean hair.

—Do you like this song? he asked.

—I love Lyle Lovett, she said.

—He's a good guy. We were at a mutual buddy's bachelor party, in Los Cabos. M.B. began nodding his head to the beat and biting his bottom lip. She could smell him. Nothing overpowering. If anything, canvas and clean dogs. She said to herself, Do you want to fuck? She laughed at that.

—What are you laughing at? he asked, laughing a little himself.

Jane shook her head. Nothing, just. Nothing.

He was all about sex. The kind who fucks in grief, or whatever middling grief you can feel over a girl who was a frayed hem. God, but Jane was not someone who fucked someone like him. Moreover, she *loved* him. She liked herself enough to love him, but she wasn't delusional. She was five-three. She had nails that grew boyishly; her hair was Indiana blond, not California blond. In cigarette pants her legs looked like cigars.

—How's the coffee? he asked, because she hadn't drunk any.

—I take milk, she said, feeling like she was riding Motocross.

—I'll raid the artists' icebox, he said. Hope you're OK with cream of wood chips.

While he was gone Jane gave herself the time to quiver. In her life she had fucked seventeen men and had been attracted to just one of them, who, she realized later, reminded her of her father. She'd been in love with multiple celebrities since she was thirteen years old. One of them had hung himself poorly and snapped his neck in his parents' garage. I would have loved you, she'd said to his picture in a magazine. His restless face, his sad, gray eyes. She marveled at how her life had only got exponentially worse.

When M.B. came back with hemp milk in a little white cup, she hadn't stopped shaking. He asked if she was cold. It was 77 degrees outside. He told her California was always like this, perfect, yellow, but he liked New York better. He had the luxury of being the most beautiful man in both places and she didn't even want to be a girl that got him. She wanted to be him.

—Jane?

It was Nicole. Who had no business being here today.

—Oh, hey, she said to M.B., great, *great* scene yesterday. I watched it on playback.

—What did you need, Nicole? Jane said.

—I need the pants. To fix a pleat.

—Uh. OK.

Nicole, who was waiting for Jane, didn't move. She wore a muslin dress, heavy and short, and gladiator sandals. She was thick and boring and in that moment Jane felt the best she'd felt in a long time, even though she knew it was artificial. The women walked inside the house together. Jane unzipped her duffel bag and brought out the khaki pants. Nicole pointed to the T-shirt inside the bag.

—Just give them both to me, she said, and I'll hand them off to him later.

Jane shook her head.

—Why not? said Nicole. What is the deal? Then she smirked. Her cold coral hand was on Jane's duffel bag.

Jane didn't know where the next thing came from. Maybe from her father's Cadillac, where as a girl she woke from a nap on her mother's lap just in time to hear her aunt, sitting beside them, say, She has such a big nose for a girl. Maybe it came from there, or an accumulation of theres.

—I'm going to sleep with him, she said.

—What? Shut up. Everybody wants to sleep with him.

—Yes, but I actually will.

She zipped up the duffel and brought it back outside with her. She was tired of people touching her things, of looking over her shoulder at her cell phone. She was tired of needing money. She'd not had enough for a nice casket. She got one from overnightcaskets .com, with a pink crepe interior. The shipping was free and the customer service representative messaged her that funeral homes had to accept caskets from outside sources, no matter what they told her. It was a federal law.

M.B. cupped his camp mug in his hands, like he was sitting around a fire. What am I wearing today?

—A Nehru shirt, said Jane. And like, these bell-bottom things. Nicole is adding a few more sashes.

—*What.*

Jane smiled. She sipped her milky coffee. Her eyes were wide open. She was so *awake.*

———————

It was the best fifteen minutes of her life. They talked about riding horses on the beach and he was reading *Paris Spleen* and they talked about that. He was smart the way movie stars are smart. They had access to everything and nerds tweeted books at them and they ate minimalist sushi and knew how to play the piano and ride motorcycles and they had been on location in damp parts of New Zealand and they knew about earthquake safety and they listened to very good, very new music. About herself, Jane said little: that she loved TRX, even though she hadn't done it in over a year. Her stomach was soft from too many bagels, but at least she walked all over the city, and she told him about her favorite block, in Chinatown. He'd never been there. She kept trying to find something stupid about him, something boring. Any gaps in his knowledge were filled by his sexuality, which he radiated like a space heater. It was unbelievable.

The sun had moved right over their Bedford garden. Jane noticed for the first time the petunias in flowerpots. They looked like little girls.

—Jane!

It was the AD, the twat. I hope, thought Jane, your husband is fucking someone two decades younger than you right now. I hope he is so happy.

—Yeah?

—Where's Matt's cardigan?

—The blue one? We don't need it till tomorrow, I thought?

—Trib wants to do a pickup later. Matt had greens in his tooth. Where the fuck is it?

Jane's whole life was about continuity. If the dress an actress wore in a previous scene was at the prop warehouse, Jane could send a PA to go get it no problem, but the AD would scream, We have to be out of here by eight; that dumbshit won't get back until six because she doesn't know how to hail a fucking cab; that leaves us only one hour to shoot because it takes an hour to break down. And Jane would want to say, *It wouldn't take an hour to break down if every one of us worked. If fucking Ricky and fucking Dante weren't checking Venmo to see if some douchebag who'd bought their Xbox sent the deposit.*

Jane took a deep breath and said to the AD, It's at the dry cleaner. Just on Bleecker. I can go get it.

The AD sighed. She'd been coddled, assuaged, but she wanted heads. That was the problem with unhappy women. They didn't just want the problem solved. They wanted everyone to die, including themselves.

—I'll go with you, M.B. said. I could use a walk. To the AD he said, Can you let Trib know? We'll be back before show time.

———————

They left like bandits. He put on a baseball cap and sunglasses. They walked close, shoulders skimming like sixth graders.

At Abingdon Market he bought two coconut waters—a special brand, they were less than four ounces each—and handed her the opened one. Crossing Perry, he thrust an arm ahead of her chest, to protect against a speeding car. He was recognized four times. Celebrity had a way of oozing via neutral, expensive clothes, Ray-Bans, Yankee caps.

The dry cleaner was on the fine side of Bleecker, with the awnings and dachshunds. They passed Diptyque and Magnolia and Lulu Guinness. He pointed to Marc Jacobs and said, I applied for a job there. I heard the manager hired good-looking guys. For a while I just went around to all these places where they hired good-looking guys.

—So you didn't get the job? Jane said.

—No, I got the job.

She said that the randomness of Hollywood was gutting to her. How could he handle it?

—It's not fair, he said, until it's still not fair, but then you're the one benefiting from the unfairness.

—So maybe in the end, she said, it all gets fair.

—Exactly, he said.

As they neared their destination a terrific nausea brought up the saliva from behind her molars. She couldn't go on living regular, having tasted this. She remembered pictures of him in Capri at a restaurant named Aurora, with an actress who she'd thought then was too plain for him, for whom she now wanted to cry.

—I have Fischl's *The Welcome*, she said. I saw the picture of Petra in front of it on your Instagram today.

He stopped and moved under a scalloped awning, out of pedestrian traffic. Jane followed.

—I don't know. I thought. That maybe. If I'd been close with her, if I could afford to, I'd give it to her mother or something.

—You have that painting?

—Yes.

He wanted to know how, of course. How could a prop master have a precious work of art. How could a Fischl live on the Lower East Side. Last week Jane sat on the floor eating corn kernels from a can and stared up at it. She'd been thinking, I need a little payoff. Something to stop me from something. She'd looked at the Fischl for guidance. A piece so valuable was better than her. She figured it knew more.

—And you're looking to sell it?

—I hadn't thought that far. I don't know what to do with it. It was a gift.

—Just recently somebody gave it to you?

—No, a year. Two years. A year and a half.

—And it's—

—In my house. My apartment. On Orchard.

He nodded. His neck. Even if you cut off his head, his neck had tongues and eyes of its own.

You could maybe come and see it. To my apartment.

He said he was free that evening. He took down her address and her phone number. An ambulance *awayoed*. Everyone died, Jane knew, but especially when you were too close to what nobody had promised you. Especially then.

———————

Five p.m. Pre-dusk late summer Manhattan. Pink like San Diego, blue and swan cream like Paris. Holy if you're happy.

Jane showered as close to his arrival as possible. She put on white lace panties and a bra, a set she'd bought at Journelle months ago. The tags were still on; she pulled the plastic free with her teeth.

She opened a bottle of Riesling. She wished she could drink vodka. She had a special edition holiday bottle of Belvedere, another gift. It was in the freezer with the end-of-days peas and chopped spinach. She poured the wine into a glass with ice and it made a cracking sound. Outside her window she could see men working on the building across the street. Their dark pants were stained with paint. But they weren't working. They'd stopped to look at her. She was in a pair of jeans and just the bra. She thought it wouldn't be so bad to be looked at like this, she wouldn't mind, if she got paid a nominal fee. A quarter or something, like a lemonade stand. She would walk down the street all day, frowning, so they all could remind her to smile.

M.B. texted, saying he was making a quick stop and would be ten minutes late. Did she have a large sauté pan?

She plugged his full name into her phone.

She opened her broken pantry door. Not only did she have a sauté pan; she had a ten-piece All-Clad set. Brand-new, shining. She was a saver. The beauty was, she'd been saving the pots and pans for precisely a night like this. Delicately, she placed a stockpot and a saucepan on the stove. The lids tingled. The stove looked suddenly aspirational. God, she was delirious. She was trembling. She went to look at the Fischl. She understood what the dead model meant, wanting to be that woman. But you could only see the woman from the back. From the back she looked peaceful, but that's easy, from the back.

She wrote, *Yes.* On the screen it looked like, *Oh, fuck yes.*

She switched on her little old iPod, connected to a battered little player, and toggled to her Brazilian mix, which she'd often played, dreaming of this very thing happening. Since she'd started working on the movie, before he was even definitively cast for the role, she'd been imagining this. The impossibility!

Moving to the beats of the atabaque, Jane felt the most sensual she'd ever felt. She brought out the San Daniele prosciutto she'd purchased on the way home with her last twenty dollars for the week. And the baguette that she'd buttered with Delitia. She hadn't had enough for cheese.

She was always thinking of a time, five to ten years in the future. A sum of money not exorbitant but comfortable—the price of a used Bentley—that would be enough to hire someone to go through her father's things, to organize all the boxes in the storage facility she could barely afford, to go through the field hockey trophies and lipstick samples and tell her it was time to toss the World History notebook, the tax returns from 2003.

It was easier to tell people that something was for money rather than love. You could move across the country for a low-paying internship. You could not do the same for a man who didn't expressly send for you.

The buzzer rang. He was downstairs, at the base of her shitty walk-up. Next door there was a hipster pickle place. Every morning it smelled like piss, and, by afternoon, like vinegar.

===

—This is delicious, he said.

Fuck you, she thought, because she hated him already.

He held a corner of baguette with the lemony butter from Parma. He chewed and walked around the apartment. He'd come with a brown bag of food. Osso buco, carrots, celery, tomato paste, broth. When he stayed in hotels, he said, he missed cooking too much. He hadn't asked if she was a vegetarian, but now he did. She wasn't, but would have eaten the veal regardless.

The Fischl was in her bedroom. Her bedroom's walls were salmon colored and lumpy. Her father's crucifix hung above her bed. Otherwise, only a black chest of drawers. Somehow it was timeless in there, a Mexican brothel. He could fuck anyone, though. He could go outside and tap a lady on the shoulder, any age, married, whatever. Women would find the nearest car hood.

—I really appreciate this, he said, slinging a dish towel over his shoulder and prepping the ingredients. He'd swapped out her iPod for his phone, playing music of a kind she'd never heard before. Jazz-rap-blues-soul-folk. The artist sang of revolution, incarceration, and mass betrayal. She imagined stark Caribbean landscapes and felt like expired vanilla ice cream.

—What? said Jane.

—Letting me cook for us. Are these brand-new?

—Yeah, um, I just got them a few weeks ago.

—And you haven't used them yet? You go out to eat a lot?

—Well, it's New York, Jane said, and felt instantly stupid.

He was securing the veal with cooking twine. His hands were elegant but manly. He moved gracefully. He told her he had an Ashtanga practice, and they talked about that for a while. In order to take her eyes off him she concentrated on the raw veal. Two pieces, the size and shape of human hearts, that smelled menstrual.

—How old are you? he asked. The question was shocking. She was younger than him, but too old. When she looked back at her history, it seemed like one year she was forbidden to light matches, playing with Barbie dolls, and bouncing rubber pink balls over jacks, and the next year she was fucking.

—Twenty-nine, she said. She was thirty-one.

He nodded. He inserted some sprigs of thyme into the marbled flesh.

—How old are you?

—Thirty-six. Shit. I'm gonna be thirty-seven in like a week.

—Thirty-six is a great age for a man, she said. But thirty-seven is old.

Her stomach growled. She hadn't realized how hungry she was. M.B. pretended not to hear. She wished she could film him moving around her kitchen, because she was unable to enjoy it in the moment. It was surreal. He wore the softest-looking pants she had ever seen. Her desire lived on multiple levels. She wanted to play Candy Land with him. She wanted to be eaten. Self-mutilatingly, she thought of the dead model. Spider legs, lonely mascara.

She said, Do you want to see the Fischl?

—After dinner, he said, as though she lived in a multiroom estate.

The osso buco took forty-five minutes. He said it usually took an hour and a half, but he'd sped it up. High heat, tight lids. He'd worked as a sous chef in his hometown in New Mexico. The line about speeding up the cooking probably cored her more than both hours of her father's wake.

They ate at her weak little table. There was a folded piece of paper towel jammed under the shortest leg. He said he could show her something better for that. That he would bring it "next time." She traveled through the course of that phrase, up the swollen canopy of the Amazon, into the clouds, then back down into the snake broth river.

They drank the bottle she'd opened. He hadn't brought one. She wondered if he hadn't because he'd expected her to have, at the least, three bottles above a microwave. Or because he hadn't planned on making it a long evening.

He washed all the pans, every single one, and dried them. The dish towel on his shoulder was the most erotic thing she had ever seen.

—Sorry I scratched up one of the pans, he said. It's because I didn't have a rubber spatula.

—It's my fault for not having a rubber spatula.

He glanced over her shoulder.

—The Fischl is through here, Jane said, without turning around.

She led him into her bedroom. They stood side by side and regarded it. Their shoulders were not touching, but both shoulders wanted to. Jane felt a unity she had never known. It wasn't love, but it was close enough.

—It's beautiful, he said at last, and then he turned to look at her. His eyes were hazy with desire. She parted her lips on purpose. She thought of the costume designer, more than anything else. While she was with a man she thought of women. It wasn't until after the man left that she thought of him. She wondered if it was only her who was like this. M.B. leaned in and kissed her. It was the kind of tongue dicking you only saw in pornography. But this was burnished. He was a movie star. He kissed like one. And smelled like one—divine nothing.

Jane had forgotten how, when sex was right, it deployed itself, like a windup dog. It skittered and found its own path. They moved onto the bed. They made out like kids for what felt like a very long time but was actually only five minutes. Her jeans felt tight. She unbuttoned them and wriggled out, saying, My pants are too tight. He laughed and said so were his, and he did the same. He undressed completely, like a god. Around his neck he wore a string of wooden beads, and he took these off and set them gently on the floor. She took off her shirt, and there she was in the white set she'd bought, with just this fantasy in mind. He brought his mouth down between her legs and it was the most movie star thing about him. She bucked and he said, Ow, careful, you almost took out a tooth.

That hurt her feelings more than she could have imagined. She thought of the last woman he had fucked—had it been the dead model?—and the next woman he would fuck, who would be more beautiful than her.

He came up and aligned himself with her. It was huge. A male friend of hers had once told her, Never tell a guy he has a big dick. Ever.

—Oh my god, she said. Jesus.

He laughed. Are you clean? he asked.

Her eyes widened. Are *you*?

—Yeah, he said. But if you're nervous.

She pointed to the black chest of drawers. Top one, she said. He went and retrieved a condom. He unfurled it, but it only went down halfway.

—Wow, she said. He shrugged, smiled, and kissed her while he put it in, one tree ring at a time. What went on for the next half hour she would remember only in rosy bursts. It was like a movie, the soft-core handsome kind that is less sexual than legendary. The first five hundred times it went in, it felt like the first time. There was no drug on earth, Jane knew, no man on earth, like this. The model knew it. Maybe that was half the reason she was dead.

After, he stood up and looked out the window. The full length of him naked was too much. He put his beads back on, and stretched out his long, bronze arms. The workers across the airway were nowhere to be found. It was just beyond sunset. Jane was under the covers.

—That was amazing, he said. You know how when you meet someone, sometimes you just feel it right away, that it will be amazing?

She nodded and swallowed air.

—*Fuck!* he said, for emphasis. Then he picked up his watch. I've gotta run. I'm supposed to meet Trib back at the hotel.

He picked up her jeans, folded them, laid them on top of her chest of drawers. It was her father, and not her mother, who had done all the laundry in her childhood home. She wanted to tell him.

After he'd dressed he came back to the bed and kissed her deeply. Don't get up, he said. Stay. He said this as though it were her dream, to lie there in a down grave while he went out into the world.

—I'll come back tomorrow? If that's OK? I'd like to buy the painting. My manager needs to make out a check.

Jane looked terrified.

—Is that OK? You do want to sell it, right?

She imagined rolls of fifties and twenties. Stocking up on pasta, hundreds of tubes of bucatini and tins of *pomodori pelati* in case she didn't make any money for a year. She could eat spaghetti every night, drink wine, bundle up.

—Yes, she said finally. Yes, I want to sell it.

—Great, he said. Jim Harris is looking into the price for me. I want to give you a good price. He winked. She nodded. He was out the door moments later.

In the morning, the men at work were back at work. She was naked, but did not feel stretched or gross. Only completely empty, in love. It was worse this way. Still, she was changed for the better. She looked at the men squeegeeing the windows, painting cornices. Not only were they poor like her, but their wives had never fucked a movie star. There was room for hope.

It was a Saturday and her neighborhood was pimply with boys in black backpacks. Jane knew she'd spend the whole day in preparation: shaving, waxing, brow tinting. But for the first hour of the morning she stayed in bed. On her phone, for which a payment was now five days delinquent, she read an article called "Thirty Times a Celebrity Didn't End Up with Another Celebrity." She called up scenes of M.B. kissing women on film and masturbated to them. She had to keep rewinding and playing, because the movies were all PG-13 and none of the scenes lasted long enough. She didn't shower, and wished he hadn't used a condom. Now she only had the parched trail of rubber inside her, instead of him.

Later, on the sunny street, she bought an iced coffee with coffee ice cubes. She paid in all quarters and dimes. Flashes of their sex flitted through her brain like subliminal advertisements. One scene, in particular. M.B. suspended above her, saying, Open your mouth. Then spitting in her mouth. A hot, round, clear drop of him dropping into the back of her throat. Their molecules fusing, his spit becoming one with her spit. It hadn't felt like a trick last night. It felt good then, and it still felt good now. She closed her eyes and imagined a bone-colored church in New Mexico. The whole way she had lived up until last night seemed like the life of someone who didn't realize she would one day grow old and die.

She passed a pop-up kiosk with a man selling plastic toys, matted dogs that flipped in the air, butterfly nets with dusty green handles. At the entrance to her building a homeless man coughed into his armpit. Upstairs, Jane counted the pills they'd given her at the hospital. She did it once a week. It was something like the superstition of not stepping on a crack or of walking under a ladder.

By three he hadn't written or called. Jane ate two slices of old turkey breast sandwiched between stale saltines. She drank green tea and set the phone to vibrate, facedown, on the kitchen table, then went into her bedroom and made the bed and went out again to check the phone, and then tucked the phone under one of the pillows and went to take a shower. She opened a jar of grapefruit scrub she'd bought six months back. She cleaned between her toes. She went back to check the phone, and there was a missed call and she cursed herself, but then she saw the missed call was from Verizon and she began to cry. Finally, there was a text from the AD saying yesterday was the last New York film day. Trib wanted to shoot the rest in the Malibu beach house. Jane would no longer be needed, but would be paid through the next week. She thought of the movie star she'd loved when she was thirteen. She thought of his neck snapping like the fine bone of a bird. She thought of her father, and missed him more than ever, and hated herself because she had not missed him at all the day before.

The door buzzer rang. She ran, naked, to the ramen-colored intercom.

—Hey, said M.B., through fuzz and air. I was in the area, so I thought I'd just stop in. Hope it's OK.

—Oh, yeah, OK. She buzzed him up and ran into the bathroom and applied mascara. Her eyelids were fat and blue. She threw on a soft sweatshirt and a pair of shorts.

He knocked on the door and she opened it, breathless. He wore running gear.

—I just got out of the shower, she said.

He walked past her. I hope I'm not interrupting.

—No.

—The stateside funeral is tomorrow. Petra's mom is going back to Mostar on Monday.

—Oh.

—It's a beautiful medieval town. Mostar. There's an old bridge that takes your breath away.

—You've been there?

—Yeah, I visited when I was filming in Italy. It's just across the Adriatic.

—Oh, so you met her mom?

—I met her mom a lot.

—Oh, that's nice. I didn't know. How close you guys were.

—Why else would you think I'd want to buy the painting?

—Um. I didn't know. Like I said, I hadn't thought that far. I just. It was a coincidence, your Instagram.

M.B. brought his thumb and index finger to the bridge of his nose. I'm sorry, he said. I'm just a little overwhelmed today. With the reality of it.

Jane thought of yesterday, when he hadn't seemed overwhelmed at all. She wished she could change coats like that. Then she realized, she had. She touched his arm with her hand, and he clamped it down with his other hand. Her heart bowled itself into her belly. He turned his face to hers. She moved her tongue into his mouth, but he gently broke away. The lobes of her intestines dropped.

He walked to the window and looked out. The workers were eating sandwiches on the rooftop. Jane wondered if their wives had packed them. The cellophane glinted like glass in the afternoon sun.

—Some days, he said, I wish I had a job like those guys. Just hanging out on some rooftop with a bunch of dudes. Clocking out at five or whatever.

—It's the weekend, Jane said. They work on the weekend.

—Yeah, so do I. And I never clock out.

Jane wanted to hurt him, kill him. It was a clearer urge than her desire.

—I love your place, he said, coming toward her. It's so cozy. He wrapped her in his arms. Hmm, and this sweatshirt is so soft, he said into her shoulder.

She wanted to tell him she loved him. She wanted to beg him. If only he knew how he could save her. There could be one less dead girl. He wouldn't have to do so much. He would have to pretend he loved her, yes, but he could fly off everywhere he wanted. He could film in Sarajevo. He could go to bachelor parties in Indonesia. She would care for his dogs. She would have a new toothbrush waiting every time.

He curled his arm around her waist and brought her pelvis into his. He moved from side to side. He inhaled the unrinsed shampoo behind her ear. She would forgive him for everything. He separated himself and held her at arm's length.

—Yesterday was our last film day.

—I heard, she said.

—I'm leaving in a few for JFK.

It was funny, Jane thought, she had already died a few times. It was funny, to keep dying.

—Do you have the papers for the painting? he said. I need to give them to Jim, and then he'll have a messenger pick it up later tonight.

Her mouth dried up, all the spit, gone. Yeah, she said, somewhere.

—No big deal, whenever, I mean, by tonight would be great. Jim said thirty thousand dollars is above fair. Is that what you heard? Is that OK?

Jane had heard forty thousand dollars. That's what the man who gave it to her had told her. She hadn't considered this happening, and hadn't called anyone. Online it said anywhere from thirty-seven to forty-two thousand dollars. But Jane had a history of overvaluing.

She nodded. Her lips parted. She kept nodding.

—OK, great. That's great. I guess it'll be nice for you to unload that piece. It's kind of a sad piece.

Jane's head became swimmy. She felt like she needed to lie down. She told him so, and he left like a gentleman.

═══════════

The next day she walked west again with the check in her hand. It would cover seventy percent of her credit card debt. Seventy percent that she would not pay, gone, like that.

The bank was so far away, on Prince, but the beauty of the block had been important to her when she opened the account.

Beautiful people came out into the sunshine. It highlighted the tone of their legs. A beautiful Black woman with a shaved head stood on the pale of her arches in a pair of clogs to kiss a beautiful Black man who leaned against the entrance to the subway. A model in shorts and ankle socks and Keds talked on the phone at an outdoor café table. Outside the old grasshopper-green façade of Vesuvio Bakery, a skinny girl in a leather skirt talked to a girl in a beautiful backless sundress. They might have woken up in filthy apartments. Perhaps their mothers didn't believe in them. Perhaps their fathers had just died. Perhaps there had been a quiet abortion down on Maiden Lane.

She passed Williams Sonoma and thought of all the new pots and pans she could buy. Le Creuset and Staub, some nice copper-bottomed ones. Any kind of pot she wanted in the whole world.

On the silver grate between a handbag store and the bank sat a homeless woman with a navy blanket across her lap. She was half in the sun, half in the stony shadow of the doorway. It was hot even in the shade, so the blanket was strange, and you didn't usually see homeless women on Prince. The woman had long hair and bangs. The color was a nutty red-brown, the kind one might hope to achieve with double process, plus highlights. She was bony, her jaw jutted, and the skin around her lips was used, like paper crumpled and unfolded and crumpled and unfolded again. Meth, Jane bet. A *venti* cup sat on an overturned United States Postal Service bin. A dollar bill periscoped out. She held a little white sign. It said she was a NEW WIDOW, NO INSURANCE, LOST EVERYTHING, CAN U HELP, EVEN 5 HELPS, GOD BLESS. She was rocking back and forth to some tune in her head. Each time she came forward her long face entered a bewitching bar of sunlight. The light changed her, at once, into something uglier and more beautiful.

—Please help, she said. Anything you can spare.

Jane walked into the bank.

PADUA,
1966

MIRANDA WAS TALL AND AS DARK HAIRED AS THEY COME. I SAY *WAS* and not *is* and that is inaccurate because she is still around and I really am not.

She wasn't exactly beautiful and as I say that I can hear the men in town hiss, scowl at me with their purple heads. Fine, she was beautiful. Is beautiful. Everybody likes a story with a beautiful woman and this one has two. Miranda had hair like soaked beetles. A big nose, the kind that looks good on a voluptuous woman. She was forty-four the last time I saw her.

And Sol was seventy-five. Still had the brick house in Mendham with the oval vinyl pool he meant to turn gunite. He talked about it every summer. Got quotes every summer. Then it turned August and he figured life passed so quickly. Besides, vinyl was soft on the feet.

Miranda was married to Luke, a WASP. They had a daughter named Caroline. A name I've never understood. He was very handsome, her husband. They had a small but nicely renovated Cape with a quarter of an acre he paid someone to mow. They fell out of love because they were never in love. He liked to get behind her and she liked the stability of a WASP, the sharp edges, clean ears, God-fearing shorts. It ended when Caroline was three. The excitement of having a child had sloughed off. The kid was like a marble countertop with water stains. This precious thing that they had to still worry over long after it lost its luster. Well, I don't think that's true of Luke. I think Luke loved the kid more than he loved himself, but you know most parents really don't feel that way. They just can't admit the opposite is true. It's the end of the world when they do.

Before it got very bad between her and Luke, Miranda used to come over and see me. Because I didn't drive she would come and pick me up and take me to Newark and we'd get veal osso buco together. Both of us Italian, we had the same tastes. More specifically, I had the same tastes of her dead mother. We would get eel, anchovies, meaty graffiti eggplants. And *struffoli*, how she loved *struffoli*! She said they were exactly the size and stickiness of childhood.

Miranda was a whore. I don't know how else to say it. The way she spoke to men, to all men. It was obscene. Fat men, old men, boys. Like her tongue was a snake. At the fish market in particular there was a Black boy. He couldn't have been more than nineteen. She eyed him and let him eye her. And more. She leaned over the counter when it came time to pay. Sometimes she paid for me. I suppose she knew then how it might come back to her. She leaned over the counter with her tan chest and her low-cut tops. The boy's name was Malcolm. It said so on his white coat. He didn't know a thing about fish.

After we went shopping we'd go for espresso. There was a place on Adams called Caffe Espresso Italia. Everybody in her group went to Starbucks, or the kinds of places that sell day-old croissants in a muggy window. But Miranda understood the importance of good coffee. My treat, she would say, almost every Sunday. Then we'd sit by the window and talk. One of the last times I saw her, she told me the story.

—I'm leaving Luke, she said. Her arm jangled with all her silver bracelets as she lifted her cup to drink.

—*Stai zita*, I said. I didn't believe her.

—No, *zia, e vero*. Sometimes she called me *zia*. I can't say it didn't warm me.

—What happened? Why?

—He's a pig, she said. This was insanity. Luke was a mouse. Everything about him you could throw in a laundry basket and forget about until the morning.

—Stop it.

—He is, *zia*. You wouldn't believe it, some of the things he wants me to do.

—What does he want you to do? I asked. Now I was interested.

She leaned into my face and whispered. Her breath was hot and wet. I could sense in that moment what it was like to be with her in that way. I heard from some people in the neighborhood she used to go with women in college. But all young people were that way now. Just pubic bones and telephones.

What she told me was lewd but by no means vile. Luke wanted to subjugate her in certain ways. He wanted to do it outside on their composite deck, in full view of the neighborhood. But in the middle of the night. While the child slept of course. Anyway, he was her husband.

—That's it? I said.

—No, she said, exhaling, as though she still smoked cigarettes. I of course did, and she would accompany me outside for them. But I wasn't one of those smokers who smoked between meals. Those idiots.

—What else?

—He hates the president. And that's fine, you know, whatever. But he's one of these, you know, these bleeding hearts.

—*Non sapevi?*

—Of course I knew a little. But no. You know this new time, it brings everything out in people.

I nodded.

—*Zia*, I just can't stand him. I hate him. I hate the way he swallows his food, you know?

I laughed. She was so young. At forty-four I had been much older than her. Perhaps I was misremembering.

—What about the kid? I said.

That is when she began to cry. Not plain tears, but torrential. I was always uncomfortable when women cried. I didn't know how to be with them. I touched her arm. It was moist. She was like a candle. Her hair smelled like smoke, mine, and her perfume. Candy smelling, cheap smelling, though probably it was engineered to smell cheap. There was so much I didn't care to understand anymore. Perhaps that's why I got sick shortly thereafter. God knows when you're done learning.

—What is it? I said.

Through her heaving tears she told me, in quiet, low-class Italian, that she didn't care about the child the way a mother should. That Caroline was better off with her father than with a mother who felt cheated by the terrific responsibility of a child. She told me that when the child cried nothing tugged in her heart. Not even when she was very sick with the flu, as she had been that winter. Even when the child's temperature shot up to 106 and Luke called the doctor in the middle of the night, trembling, Miranda said she only bided her time until she could go back to bed. She was in the habit of taking sleeping pills and she was irritated the effect was wearing off, the head clearing to make way for the fuck of day. That was the phrase she used. I have never spoken like that, although I have certainly thought in scandalous ways.

I can't say I was surprised. I knew what type of woman she was. She told me there was yet more. A man, of course, as there always must be. A Black man, she said, her voice a growl. She knew I would be stunned and she loved that I was. She said how much it turned her on to be had by a Black man. He lived only a few blocks away from the *caffe* we were in. She said, in fact, that while we had been sitting there he'd sent her a message on her phone asking if she wanted to come by to be laid. She talked about the size of him. The ebony muscles.

—What does he do? I asked. I thought of the fish boy.

She cast her thick tan neck back and laughed, hideously.

—*Zia*, God help me, I think he sells drugs.

—What?

—I mean I know he does. He sells crack cocaine. He has a cot for a bed and his bathroom is a shared one down a dirty hallway. I love to be laid in his bed. I love how I feel lying there after it's over. I feel like I'm bleeding out.

I said I needed a cigarette. She laughed and we went outside and that was when the cough started. Of course it started sooner than that, but that was when I noted it. The first time I noted it. You can sense your own mortality more in the presence of someone who has found a new bead on life.

———————

I would like to tell you, if you care to know it, that I never learned to drive. I came to this country and I never got behind a wheel. One of my first few months in the States I was talking to some girlfriends on a stoop in Orange. We were all smoking cigarettes. Some of us had children and on those afternoons when our husbands were at work we ran out of things to do by midday. In the summer the parks were too hot, the streets were too hot. Nowadays in July and August you can't find any mothers in their hometowns, trying to fit their children's bodies into hot metal swings. They are all at the beach, at the lake. Their families have houses somewhere with an ocean breeze, or they have cousins in Colorado with money and multiple bedrooms. Back when I was young it wasn't like that and this one afternoon we were all smoking our long, thin cigarettes on the porch until suddenly this egg-colored VW bus pulled up on the curb. Behind the wheel was a woman. Back then we would have called her a broad. She had muscles like a man and denim coveralls with the sleeves crudely cut off at the elbows.

—Ladies and children, she called out her open window, I've got a one-way shuttle to Atlantic City. Climb aboard!

We laughed. Some of our children jumped for joy. We didn't know who she was or what was happening, but we got on that bus. All four of us, with five toddlers between us. We gave her money for gas and we stopped for cool drinks and drove down to Atlantic City, smoking and hooting out the window. When the shoulders of the highway began to fill with sand, I began to feel a pulse in my wrist.

And I met a man that afternoon, on the boardwalk. I had dropped my purse and he picked it up and that's how things used to happen. Magic. We walked together from one end to the other. He said he was a sailor but was dressed like a fisherman. We drank Lime Rickeys and ate raw oysters from a stand on a pier. I had never before eaten an oyster raw and I never would again. We did not make love under the boardwalk. We did not talk about husbands. We did not ask each other's names. It was the only day I did not feel like the person I had left behind in my little village.

That was the feeling Miranda inspired in me. She was not a good person, but she did good for me the day that she told me her story. She reminded me of my old pulse. I watched her leave, to go and meet the drug dealer down the road. I caught a bus home. My face was flushed like a schoolgirl's. I felt normal. Nobody can tell me there is a better feeling in the world.

There came a soggy fall afternoon. The kind that feels stately, that even if you live in a not-beautiful place, the streets seem to glow with elegance. The leaves smelled dead in that very pungent way that is almost the opposite of death.

Miranda, by then, was moved out of the little Cape and the rumor about town was that she was addicted to drugs and living in Newark, under the bridge. Luke had got fully custody, but then Miranda had not even shown up at the court. It was only in the past few weeks that people said she'd started coming around again, but nobody knew for sure. She was like a ghost. Linda Valenti, who lived next door, said she saw Miranda come after suppertime. Luke only cracked the door, would not let her in, would not budge an inch. Linda said Miranda must have lost fifty pounds. She was a twig. Her big black hair was thin and looked gray. She was screaming about her child. Let me see my little girl, she hollered down the middle-class streets. Linda said the whole block could hear it, and that's when another woman said she had, in fact, heard a wailing. It was terrible, someone else suddenly agreed. The sound of a mother who missed her blood. You could not feel nothing for someone who had made a terrible mistake.

But it wasn't until that damp afternoon that I saw her myself.

The day she came to see Sol. She knocked on the door loudly, then softly. She did look sickly, but she still had her breasts. Her neck was still thick. Her hair, in the dark fall light, was not gray but the same terrific licorice everyone always went on about.

He invited her in. She'd brought *struffoli* and a bottle of Cynar. They sat at the rosewood table in the dining room that was never used. Sol was very fat by this time. He was a doctor but an old one and old doctors were permitted to be fat. He was bald and pale but had an intelligent look to him, even when he was breathing heavily.

She told him the story, everything except she left out the drugs and the color of the man she went with. It was over between them. He hit her in the mouth with his ringed hand. She showed Sol the spot where the tooth was gone.

Sol leaned forward and held her face in his hand, surveying the damage. He said he had an oral surgeon friend who would fix it for her. Miranda was grateful. He poured them two glasses of Cynar and said he had not seen *struffoli* in forever.

After some time Miranda began to cry and said she missed her child. That there was a pit in her heart. She was wearing a burgundy romper. Her legs were still brown and big. Sicilian blood works like the sun, tanning the flesh from the inside out. She consoled herself that Caroline, the child, was better off without her. But still, in the middle of the night her breasts ached for the child. Her whole body. She didn't have money to get her own place. She couldn't get partial custody without her own place. Luke wouldn't let her even see the kid, the way she was now. Penniless. She was sleeping at the house of a woman she knew, indeed under the bridge, and at night the noise was so bad, the train and the screams, and it smelled like the kind of piss that was not merely old but diseased. Not like in Italy, she said, where the piss smells beautiful. Sol smiled.

—You miss your kid, Sol said.

—So fucking much, I feel like not just my heart, but like my lungs are torn out.

She pulled at the skin between her chest viciously.

—Sorry, Sol.

He shook his head. She asked him what he thought.

—Let me tell you a story, Sol said. About a beautiful woman.

Miranda leaned forward. Beautiful women loved the stories of other beautiful women. They felt they could learn from them.

—When I was completing my residency in Padua, I did my homework every night in this little *caffe*. I drank espresso, then switched to wine around seven, and the owner would give me whatever pasta they had a surplus of. There was a waitress there. The most beautiful woman I had ever seen, with black hair that dipped down below her rear. Like yours, maybe even thicker. She was twenty-six, old to be unmarried in those days. I only watched her from afar for a long time. I was a busy young man, learning not only medicine but Italian at the same time.

—Forgive me, Sol, but why go to medical school in Italy if you don't know Italian? Besides being attractive, she had that other quality that women like her had. They knew which questions to ask. They knew the right questions all the time.

—My family couldn't afford medical school in the States. It was free in Italy back then, paid for by the government. All you had to do was practice at night in the hospitals. All night long, sometimes.

—That's a lot of hard work to do.

—It was. Yes. Men these days don't put the time in. You have to put the time in when you are young. And these days. Well, you know.

They both laughed, because Luke was a writer.

—When my last semester was over, I took her out. She was a very quiet woman. Of course we barely spoke the same language.

—Did you have her right away, the first night?

Sol smiled, the corned smile. All men have one, even the fattest and the kindest.

—No, he said. The second one. And he winked.

—Mind if I smoke? Miranda said.

Sol got up. His largeness, it was like a prehistoric bird. He picked up an ashtray from the Albergo Lungomare in Rimini and set it on the rosewood table that was polished to a high shine. There was a hole in one of the windows of the hotel the ashtray was from and one morning he'd woken to find a crow at the foot of the bed. Staring. The crow was larger than the hole in the window.

He took out a pack of cigarettes from the drawer of the armoire and lit her up with a 1930s Dunhill that had a deco swing arm.

—Beautiful, she said.

—Isn't it.

—So how was it?

—It was wonderful, he said, but in that way men have where they aren't thinking about the past. In prurient matters, men always live in the present. The past is just the fluffer. Of course in all other matters, sports and cars and presidents, men live in the past. I wish I could say I didn't somehow admire it.

He proceeded to tell her the rest of the story, the lame leg of it. How the beautiful waitress had a child, a two-year-old for whom she could barely provide. Sol was almost done with school by the time he'd taken her out. He was set to go back to the States. His grandmother had recently passed and left him a good chunk of money to start his own practice; perhaps there would be enough left over to buy a house. But he was Catholic; his mother was a hard, hard woman. She painted little girls inside seashells but never laughed or smiled. He could not bring over a bride with a child by another man. He could not.

Miranda sucked gluttonously on the cigarette. It was a Marlboro Red 100, left over from a stale soft pack.

—What happened?

—She came with me, he said softly. Before we left she set the child down, as it slept, inside the town chapel. Set it on the altar a few minutes before the mass would start. I gave her a roll of bills that she tucked inside the child's blanket. We left for America. You know the rest.

—Jesus Christ, Miranda said. She drank down the rest of her Cynar.

—So you see, Sol said.

Miranda shook her head. Maybe she did, and maybe she didn't. She crushed out the cigarette. When she was done Sol covered her hand with his own.

—You have a problem, Miranda. I see it. You've had a hard life. Don't think I don't understand.

She nodded her big head, her full head of hair.

—What can I do?

—What can any of us do? Sol said, looking deeply into her eyes. His hand was big and pale over hers. He didn't see how badly hers wanted to get out from under his. I have always wondered how some men are able to unsee such things. But like the crow in the hotel room that morning, Sol was able to make sense of it, one that fit the math in his own head. Me, I knew the crow for what it was. That was the night, after all, that I made my decision, in that hot room with the ocean across the street and the boys hollering at the girls at the *gelateria*.

Miranda started to cry. These were not the heaving tears I'd seen. These were the quiet, beautiful tears that beautiful women cry in front of unattractive men. They are not clear these tears but blue like sea glass. If you tasted them you would find them salty and hard.

—I can help you, Miranda, Sol said. And his voice turned throaty, filled with wetness and trees. I mean, he said, that I can help you with money. Here and there.

He took her hand and brought it toward his giant legs. He wore huge and ghastly khaki shorts. The kind from the cheap department stores that men even older than himself shopped in. Pathetic, for a doctor, but of course after I was gone he had no one to shop for him. I had been unable to have any children. Everyone said it was a pity, and everyone didn't even know the whole truth.

I can only see when the lights are on and the lights soon switched off and I stopped looking in for some time. Even after you stop wanting to learn, there is yet a greater boredom you can feel with life. *Boredom* is perhaps not the right word, but I don't know the word in English. The last thing I saw was the *struffoli* on the table. He'd plated them in a bowl I brought from the apartment I shared with my child. It was the only thing I brought to this country, and I am, if you care to know, sad to leave it.

GRACE
MAGORIAN

OH BLOODY FUCK, THOUGHT GRACE MAGORIAN WHEN SHE SAW the two of them coming toward her at the starter.

The girl was twenty-seven to thirty-two, that pitiful age when unmarried women became Cujos beneath their thin, bronze skins.

The boy was the same age. Dark haired and bearded, wearing a sleeveless shirt and nice. No. Wonderful arms. Like a sailor. But of course not. These days, especially in America, men got their muscles at the gym. On the Nautilus. Muscles grew out of air conditioning. And the boys got their clothes at the gyms, too, these fancy gyms. Grace was fifty. All right, fifty-one. She'd never belonged to a gym back in Galway, but here she'd joined a Lucille Roberts once upon a time. Most recently she'd started up again at a Healthworks Fitness Center for Women. Everything was mauve, rubbery. No men, nothing harder than a lump of cancer in the place. But she felt comfortable. She wore her Goatboy Soaps top and her bleach-stained Lycra pants and on Saturday evenings she swam in the pool, whole place to herself, taking long luxurious breaststrokes through the green, palmy water.

Everything she did, come to think of it, was to avoid being in the same places as these two, with their sunglasses and their brunch elbows.

Today of all days. She'd wanted to treat herself. Mother's Day. The golf course was her sacred place. Generally she came on weekdays, at odd times, to avoid being paired with eejits like these. A certain type. Well, what were they? They were young, is what they were. The boy could get hard anytime.

It wasn't really so much about Mother's Day. Or that she'd been paired with these two. It was that she had been *paired* with *two*. Instead of *one*—a man, with a nice swing, smile. A widower, a divorcé. With children, without. Didn't bloody anyfuck longer matter. Because the truth was everything Grace did was to fall in love. Even since she'd stopped trying to meet someone. In fact, *especially* since she'd stopped trying. The stoppage itself was the final crusade, the last line of troops she'd sent out into the tick grasses of May.

—This is our second date, the girl whispered to Grace while the boy was teeing off. The girl didn't know not to talk at all in backswings.

Oh? said Grace, silently, with her face.

—We met on Venus, the girl said. Her face was conspiratorial. Very pretty, dark hair. The kind you could do anything with, barrettes, half ponytails. Grace's hair was fan-fiction red, gorgeous, if difficult to wrangle and dry. No man had ever dreamed his fingers through it. Not even the air force pilot with the Alsatian.

The boy struck the ball well. His body remained curved in the aftermath of his stunning shot. The landscape—a heady mix of glorious Irish links and burnished New World—accordingly froze all around him. They'd imported the very particular fescue from the damp meadowlands of North Africa. It rung the white hazards like

troll hairs. Otherwise the lawn was emerald Bermuda and the club-
house was a cube of imposing, shining glass, where good lawyers
went when they died, plus a two-hundred-thousand-dollar view of
the Statue of Liberty and the boats in the harbor of Port Liberté.

—It's a dating app, the girl continued now, louder, where the
men have to get in touch first, but they can only write to three women
per week. And those women have to neg the guy before he can move
on to the next woman. Or, if none of them respond for forty-eight
hours, he can move on.

—What's the draw then? Grace asked, as the boy returned to
them, triumphant. Great shot, she said to him.

—Sorry? said the girl.

—For the men? Grace said. Why would they use the service at all?

The boy was the type who listened. Perhaps he liked this girl.
Grace always figured all men didn't like the women they were with.
It was how to get through a day.

—Easy, the boy said, clasping both his hands—one white gloved
the other tan—on the shoulders of the brunette. Quality women.

The girl blushed.

—It's invitation only, she said. You have to be invited to join, and
even then you're vetted. IQ, personality, career.

Career, Grace thought. Grace was the estate manager for a family
of the kind of absurd wealth you did not believe until you saw. The
Hoppas. The husband was a stockbroker, nothing wild, but the wife
was the heiress to a certain mustard empire. She'd gone to Brillant-
mont in Lausanne. Once she had golden pigtails and now she cried
to a black-and-white photo of her mother each night, backlit and
trenchant on her vanity. Around the frame was a squadron of Kewpie
dolls, bare bummed, masonic.

Estate manager. A nice title. All that Grace did for the Hoppas she couldn't say out loud. Some of it was so shameful, she might as well be flossing their cracks after they took shits in their dual marble baths.

—I see, said Grace. Well, how nice for you it's working out.

—With everything going on these days, the girl said, you need a third party to make sure a guy isn't rapey. Venus takes care of all that.

When the girl walked to the women's tees, the boy asked Grace Magorian if she were married. Grace could be forgiven for thinking there was some mild flirtation to it. He was a charming type, generous with physical closeness. He picked up her clubs, held the flag when she putted. She was happy there weren't any around like him who'd fought for their countries, who had any proper manhood bumping about. It would be much harder that way.

—No, she said. Never married. She added the second part because it was either you added it straight off or you lied. Had she lied, she'd hate herself all night. She might not even take herself out for the Mother's Day sushi dinner she'd been planning. Blue Ribbon! She had a gift card from some millionaire friend of Mr. Hoppa, whom she'd helped out in a titanic way last summer. Seventy-five dollars. It was a nice-enough amount, if you were dining alone.

—Well, said the boy, you have a really beautiful accent.

—————

When Grace Magorian got home she drew herself a bath. Home during the summer—and most holidays—was the Hoppa estate in Bridgehampton. She had a room of her own in the service wing, with the housekeeper and the caretaker. But the rest of the year it was a studio on Jane Street. The Hoppas lived in a flabbergasting penthouse on Charles, and they wanted Grace close, so they rented her a small space in a brick walk-up. From her window perch she could watch the mademoiselles pour out of the bars, catch a whiff of them, too. Vodka and sunshine.

In the subterranean wood and stone den, she was seated at a table by the bar. All twosomes at the bar, boy girl boy girl, and the girls were all brunettes. Everywhere these days, all you saw was dark hair and faces the color of the cashew milk they glugged.

Grace had brought *Anna Karenina*. She was on page 44. One time, at a little wine bar on Elizabeth, a man saw her reading *A Bend in the River* and sent her over a double of the Scotch she'd been drinking. He was an Aussie paramedic, with a wide, rowdy neck and blue eyes. They shared some laughs and went to bed. Between her legs, his tongue was a diamond cutter. Come with me to Paris, he said. I'm leaving in the morning. Yes, she said. Yes, yes.

That was seven years ago, and she still brought books to dinner.

Her friend Talia—Hebrew, vicious—told her she was still single because she wasn't enough of any one thing. She wasn't frank enough or reserved enough, didn't drink too much or not at all, was neither rich nor poor; even the weight of Grace Magorian was rackingly moderate—she was neither skinny nor heavy, not busty nor flat. In all departments, Grace was in the middle. Talia was single, too. But Talia got regularly legless on ouzo. Talia went on more dates, she pointed out to Grace Magorian. You see? she said. I am who I am. I am remembered.

—Yes, Grace said. Yes, yes.

From the female (fuckit!) waitress, Grace ordered *uni, ikura, unagi,* sea bream, *aji, botan ebi,* amberjack, and jellyfish. She ordered a large sake as well as a plum wine that came in a perfect wooden box.

Halfway through her fish a man sat at the bar, much younger than she, alone and in a herringbone suit. It used to be that it would take a special sort to get it up in her. A man on the subway, autumn haired. She'd fantasize the whole ride about the life they could have, sheepdogs in the countryside. Now it was barely love she clung to. Merely the idea of not dying alone. Merely that. She was considering lesbianism. They took older women.

Grace's eyes were crossed with liquor, but this man at the bar, he looked familiar. She cocked her head, squinted. It was, indeed, the young man from the course.

—Hello! she said.

Half the room looked up from their conversations. But not the man himself. So Grace Magorian stood herself up, closed the distance.

—Well, hello there! she said.

The man blinked, and then he recognized her.

—Oh, hey, he said. He was a little surprised, not entirely happy.

—Well, this is quite the coincidence!

—Isn't it? Yeah. Crazy. Holy shit. Then he looked down at his phone, and drunk or not, Grace was no fool.

—Well, I'll leave you to it, she said.

—Grace, right? the boy said.

—Grace Magorian.

—You're here alone?

—Yes.

—I'd ask you to join me, but I have a friend coming to meet me. He lowered his voice, eyes sub-rosa: Actually another friend from Venus. Where I met Veronica.

Grace nodded. Oh, she said. I see. No worries, none at all, I'm off to my little corner of the world.

—I just meant like. Don't blow my cover, ha. You know young women these days; if they figure you're dating other people, they wake up the next day all *hashtag me too* and shit.

Of course, ha-ha.

She began to amble away, but something stopped Grace Magorian, and she doubled back.

—Jed, she said. He was in the middle of composing a text to somebody named Homeland Security.

—Yeah?

—Actually, I have a favor. Rather strange, left field, I suppose. Wondering if you might. If it's not a trouble. Invite me to that site of yours. If it's not just for young people. If you might, then I could.

—Ha-ha, he said. What's your email?

Grace gave it.

—No problem, he said, taking it down on his phone.

—Thank you.

He winked at her, in a way that made her feel exposed. She turned, attractively, with the soft, recessed lighting at her back.

The last man with whom Grace had been intimate was an architect. She'd let him come inside her, had felt the cream of him shushing against the wall of her diaphragm. He'd been beautiful, tall and gentle. Almost an apparition of a man, really, with his nice teeth and his healthy-looking body. He'd been gone, albeit politely, within the hour, never to be heard from again. What came out of her the next morning looked like paint chips.

That was three years ago. And now the world was shifting. All Grace wanted was to be loved, to be heartily fucked and unconditionally loved. She wished she had the occasion to hate that she'd been harassed. Of course she had suffered the tiny, daily rapes, and the more acute ones from her youth. But the dearth of love, there was nothing like it. The truth was she envied these women had the luxury to evoke the bad fucks and half fucks and near fucks that had wounded them. Grace struggled to remember any touch at all.

─────────

Later that evening in her pink-walled studio, Grace plugged the new mauve vibrator with the jaunty ears into her laptop and clicked around for something romantic but heathen. She found a video of a young couple on the subway, posted to an Instagram account called Beasts of New York. The girl, in a swingy, black cotton skirt, was straddling the boy, who wore velour sweatpants. The girl's face was pretty and drunky as she butter-churned on the boy's lap. His gestures were noncommittal; he was not even passionately receiving but laconically entertained. When the vibrator was sufficiently charged, Grace took her fresh laundry from the spinning dryer and went to lie down on her firm, twin bed. There she held a bouquet of clean towels to her face and the rabbit to her peach panties as the video of the amorous subway couple cycled on the laptop beside her. These days, it took twenty seconds, max. She barely needed the loop.

Afterward she lay there and thought of her father. It was best to think of one's parents directly after an orgasm, when there is so much open space.

Donal Magorian. Tall, broad in the neck and shoulders but skinny in the legs, with a pink face and red nose, hands large as irons. From the time he was nine years old, he'd cut peat and burnt turf with two Clydesdales. Later, when steel came to do the work of men, Donal and several out-of-work comrades took on a project from a foreign developer, to build a golf course in their little town. It was two years of bone-breaking work, of men in white pants coming to swing invisible clubs on a mound and determine this hill might look better just *there*. Half the crew drank itself to death, in rage but mostly enervation. The day of the rope-cutting ceremony, Donal was one of the only men left standing, as much in the foreground of the scene as a blue-collar man could be. He stood just behind a placid Armenian with a big scissor. Grace watched on the telly, a little ashamed though mostly proud. She was at home, doing her homework, dotting all the i's to ensure she'd never marry a man like her father. Because she was sure Donal Magorian was the only good, poor man in the world. This opinion was likely handed down from her mother, Frances, who loved her husband but hated their station, who'd never been to Paris, or in a car that shone. And then, while making eye contact with him on the screen, fourteen-year-old Grace watched her father strike a paw to his chest and keel over, crumple, really, like a bad gag of a heart attack. True to Irish form, the town paper said he'd died of happiness, of pride, in himself and the beauty of the course he'd helped create.

—Bollocks, said Frances Magorian. My husband died a slave. There's nothing left for us 'ere.

In a matter of weeks they'd abandoned their little flat above Mc-Donnell's Bar & Undertakers and were off with some pension money to America. It was the particular tragedy of mother-duo systems like Grace and Frances, that because the mother had never got what she needed out of life, the daughter must never advance past a certain degree. Any improvements must happen in quiet, under cover of night. And eventually even those would die the death of the undeserving, the Icaruses who had flown too close to the suburban suns of the U.S.A. Frances did find her man, a silvery American named George. She said he looked like Jimmy Stewart when he smiled. They never married, but Frances and Grace moved in with him, to his ugly but clean split-level in Cranford, New Jersey.

Just then there was a nice ding on her laptop. Grace shushed the jittery vibrator and checked the screen. *Welcome to Venus* was the subject line. She clicked a link and there were a series of easy-to-follow prompts. She wrote a brief and spry *About Me* paragraph, and uploaded a picture of herself on the links her father built, in County Mayo. The photograph was taken seven years ago. Next was the birth date, and she toggled around on the year. Nineteen sixty-six sounded like a terrific year for wine, but not for a woman to be born.

Fuckit, she thought. Like Talia said, Everybody lies these days. If you don't, you're toast. She selected 1972. Then 1973. Forty-five, she could pass for that. Really, she could. But not a minute younger. The only way to be any younger was to use even older photos of herself, of which she didn't have that many, or to use a photo of a younger woman. She considered that for a moment. Considered using fake pictures, so that at least a good man would write. That might be enough, to just be desired, even if it wasn't her actual whole self he was desiring.

She was shocked, right away, at how impressive the men were. She'd been on Match last year, remembered with choking gloom all those nights when she'd start off bright-eyed, mousing around, and, sure enough, by 2:47a.m. she would be on the eighteenth page of men forty-two to sixty-four. Feeling winded and having gone back, several times, to adjust the salary range. Grace did not care about money, but her mother had.

On Venus there were only three men per page, and Grace was being asked to rank them, so the site could better configure its algorithms to serve her. The pictures of the first three men. Grace's jaw dropped. They were kind looking, wealthy looking, no ornery eyebrows, no shirtless hicks on motorcycles. No selfies in bathrooms.

—Fuck me! said Grace Magorian. She'd found the cache! Where all the good ones had been hiding. Nearly, she texted Talia.

Where *is* everyone? Grace's mother used to ask. She'd come to America hoping to see "good people" and where were they? Were they in Aspen in the winter? The Hamptons in the summer? But some summers, they were in Nantucket! It took Frances too long. In many ways, Grace knew she'd taken the job for the Hoppas to answer her mother's question, to know *where* the good people were. And now she knew where all the good, single men were, too. She thought of all the Beaujolais she had drunk alone.

She went through a couple of pages, ranking. She was supposed to do this for 101 sets of three, or until she found what the site called *The One*, a man she wanted to message her straightaway.

She could not believe how impressive they all were. Frances Magorian used to say, All the reflective men are gay. Don't chase a dream, Gracie. Men, in her mother's estimation, were either hardworking oxen with big jaws and hearts and no brains, or else they were rich, perfect, cruel, and unattainable. How rare it is to grow up past the iniquities that ached our parents. They are little holes bored in the brain, too small to ever fill.

Outside, it began to pour. Almost immediately after she heard the first pattering, Grace's phone sounded the familiar siren. A voice memo from Mrs. Hoppa.

—Grace, did you secure the exterior door to the outdoor sauna in Bridgehampton?

Grace knew Mrs. Hoppa didn't want a voice memo back. She wrote, *Yes ma'am.* She deleted the *ma'am.* She added an exclamation mark after the word *Yes*, then deleted that, too. She added a period, and sent it.

She went back to her laptop. Please, one of you save me, she said to the screen.

And then, one of them did.

=====

His handle was DigLitt. He looked like a John. Like a man, is what he looked like. The way they used to look. The first line of his profile text read, *I am searching for the best woman in the world.*

The balance of the text was confident but not arrogant. He was not, he wrote, a metrosexual or a tough type or a brunch type or a Trump type; he was not any type; he was simply a man, his own man, and possibly yours. He was good with tools, cooking. He owned a construction company and built houses in underserved villages in South America. He'd lived and worked in thirteen countries. He knew how to read maps, and yet he always stopped to ask for directions. He believed red hair was caused by sugar and lust. Grace touched her hair, her red, red hair.

He was wealthy but not an asshole. Was this possible? Grace hadn't thought so. But here was this man. This smart, funny, alluring, six-two fifty-year-old *man*. His pictures depicted a full and varied life. Kentucky Derby with ringleted nieces. A black-and-white wedding in Rio. Making French toast in Telluride. Playing with a glorious golden retriever in Central Park. He loved William Trevor stories and raclette and Abraham Lincoln and was of Celtic descent and loved Irish dance and loved Irish accents and he loved women who could play the violin and who weren't arrogant and he loved golf and coconut water but distrusted the yoga community at large.

Her hands flew off the mouse. She was afraid. That digital fear of showing someone you love them, you are stalking them, you are watching their Instagram story seventeen thousand times in one evening. There was the button at the bottom of the page, Tell DigLitt he is The One! *(Don't worry, we won't actually tell him that, we'll just say you wouldn't mind if he borrowed your* Short History of Everything. *Then he'll have 48 hours to feel you back.)*

She touched between her legs. She felt hungry again, as though she hadn't come a mere hour earlier. She imagined John—she was sure that was his actual name—atop her. Fondly she remembered sex, the back-and-forth of it, the way it was best when it felt the man's member was slipping away, out of you. Christ, how much was inherited from her mother, the disease of her need.

In the past, Grace had felt deplorably happy when men bestowed the smallest kindnesses. If they held the door. If they absorbed their semen off her thigh with a quality paper towel. But this man. This John would love her. She could feel it.

She took a deep breath in and clicked the button.

———

In Grace Magorian's sixteenth year, she'd learned what true love was and, just as quickly, accepted that it was not for her.

Other bits of love had begun sooner, starting when she was nine or so. Instinctively she knew *love* was not the right word. Cuddling twiggles on her knee at the dinner table. The nighttime check-ins that began quietly and grew into fifteen- and thirty-minute sessions. Out her door after, she'd hear him say to her mum,

Another nightmare. Not a problem, Franny. It's my pleasure.

The thing was, what was the thing? The thing was, by the time

Grace was old enough to feel the oval notion, George was the only thing she associated it with. It made it better that he belonged to her mother. Each time Frances was cold to her, Grace had her little revenges. The first night George became her lover coincided with the week that Frances had all but forgotten her only child's birthday.

—Frig me, Grace, you're fifteen today. Feels like only yesterday we put yer big da in the ground and you held to my knees like a refugee.

Grace didn't know she was with child for three months. There was so much extra saliva in her mouth, but otherwise she felt like a regular blooming girl. She was excelling in school, had loads of friends, and was fucking her mother's boyfriend once a week. Wednesday was the special day, when Frances would go out food shopping, which she enjoyed doing alone. There was a little routine. As Frances was preparing to leave, George would shower and go to wait in his office, reclined on the faux-suede pullout, which they didn't discuss he'd bought precisely for this purpose, and reading some big, beautiful book. James Joyce, often. And when Grace sauntered in, like a less aware Lolita, George would clear his throat and begin to read aloud.

—"It was of a night, late, lang time agone, in an auldstane eld, when Adam was delvin and his madameen spinning watersilts, when mulk mountynotty man was everybully and the first leal ribber robber that ever had her ainway everybuddy to his love-saking eyes and everybilly lived alove with everybiddy else. . . ."

And Grace would go to sit beside his waist and on cue his large priestly hand would come to rest on her hip. By increments—and it was these discreet slow-building increments that she grew to associate with rocketing desire, so that for years Grace could wait on love—he would be plunging inside her, the book wedged somewhere against their still-clothed bodies. She would come again, later, to the presence of paper cuts.

By the sixth month there was no hiding it. One fall morning Grace emerged from the shower and Frances saw it, the slope of her daughter's young belly, and grabbed her by the ear. Grace said it belonged to some eejit from Irvington. A Black feller, she said, by way of accounting for some wrongdoing. Where was George? Grace could not remember those months. She had no memory of him from then, but he was not dead yet.

She was not taken to the doctor. Frances gave her black syrupy things to drink. Potions, she called them. But the fetus, who evidently had the genes of Donal Magorian, persisted.

———

In the morning, there was a single email. From *The One*, by way of Venus.

Grace's heart grew to twice its normal size. She did not open the email straightaway. First she did the three or four things she'd been dreading. She sent an email to both Hoppas, Thing One and Thing Two, asking for a raise. She paid off a credit card bill with some of her dwindling cash. She made a mammogram appointment. Then she went on Facebook and wrote to a few friends back in Ireland whom she felt warmly toward, but who thought of her as a prodigal daughter, gone to eat from silver spoons in the new world. *Hey, Angela, nice photo. How's the craic? G.*

For a few minutes Grace got lost in Angela's little, warless life. Angela had a beautiful daughter named Mary Katherine. She had red hair like her mum, and like Grace; it seemed all the girls Grace had grown up with had had red hair. Mary Katherine appeared to be single, but it wouldn't be long. She was in her late twenties, with a set of erotic tits and a rich, auburn brow.

Finally, with a cup of pine tea she'd stolen from the Hoppas' Ketchum home, Grace read DigLitt's profile again. Particularly she loved his Idea of a Perfect Day. *A farm of fresh-cut winter berries, glazed in a frost. We aren't homesteaders, but in the winter we can things, you and I, and we don't tell anyone, which is how to maintain goodness. The clouds are winter blue. Our Alaskan huskies are tired from a day of herding the miniature babydoll sheep. We take off our water-resistant winter boots that we bought in Montreal, when everything seemed free, and dry our wet feet by the fire. You heat our cider and Calvados while I clean the artichokes and later, we eat them, our faces glazed in the oil of the vegetable. I ask you to say Plum pudding, again and again and again and again. And again.*

He liked his cold to be ice-cold and his hot to be melting hot. He liked extremes in everything, his trees to be not pines in the Adirondacks, not even sequoias in Tahoe, but giants in the Yukon. He likes his women either untouched angels or deeply damaged, like a case of chilled Labatt that had been shipped without temperature control to Florida.

She opened the email. *Dear Grace,* it began.

Her heart, her red, red heart!

I am writing to say,

And then Grace's heart turned cool, into a gray liver.

The email ended there. No more text, no more signature, just a swath of white. At the very bottom, *Sent from my Venus.*

Clearly, *clearly!* There had been a whole beautiful paragraph in there, saying she was the one, too, her love of Bach and Gaddis and bidets, but he didn't realize it had got erased before he hit Send. He was worldly and had lived in Africa and was full of pulchritude and nonprofits, but he did not know how to work these newfangled dating sites and why should he!

Quickly, she wrote. *Hey hey—I received your Dear Grace, but it ended after* I'm writing to say, *and Dear John, I am writing back to say, I read your profile and Jiminy Christmas! Also your eyes are remarkable. I enjoy artichokes more than any other woman in the world. I don't know if I am the best woman in the world, but I think that I could be? Can you kindly resend what you wrote?*

═══════

When the baby, at last, had come out of her, it was plain and silky, as a rabbit in a store window. It was too early but alive, and Grace herself was so young, she didn't realize it was not too late to be saved. When Frances left the room for more towels, the wonderful thing swam to Grace's breast. It did not suckle; it was not interested in food. *She.* She was a girl. With lips like tuna belly and fingers like the springing tendrils of grapevine left to stand lonely after the harvest.

As the years burred away the glinting trapezoids of memory, Grace was left with merely the summary of the situation: In another life, Grace Magorian lost a child. A miscarriage in the seventh month. Back in Ireland, was it? No, no. Here, in the States, and yet, a late, lang time agone. And remember. Women like her did not make a big deal. The type of women men found the easiest to be around, and yet did not marry.

At noon there was a ding at her computer. But it was not from the love of Grace Magorian's life. It was an email from the Hoppas. From Thing One, the missus.

Dear Grace, Thank you for your email, our account manager has

advised against a raise, but we will talk about it some more. Would you
have the freon checked in Bridge, we never got properly cooled last night.
We are on our way back into city. See you—Mrs. H.

They liked Grace to be in whichever house they were not occupy-
ing. Grace packed her bag. It would be good to be in the Hamptons.
The love of her life would feel her distance and he would seek her out
faster. It was necessary, of course, to play games in the very beginning.

———

The kitchen of the house in Bridgehampton was a kitchen for astro-
nauts, for moon boots and bottomless bowls of lemon. Azul Macau-
bas counters and steel that shone like guillotines.

Grace had brought artichokes from the city. They were charred
at the tips but otherwise sumptuous. She set them on the counter,
with two bottles of claret. Grace had stopped smoking in 2004, but
sometimes she forgot, and looked for a light. It had been two days.
He had not written.

She knew, if the whole weekend passed without word, that she
would write again. But that she already knew this was hurtful enough
to make her hate him. Already he was cruel. Already, once again, her
life was over.

But he wasn't cruel. He did Habitat for Humanity. He did not
merely go to charitable parties but built houses with his own hands.
He'd watched every single episode of *Sex and the City*.

I am searching for the best woman in the world.

Grace remembered, with bitter fondness, the time her mother
said to her, Who do you think you are in that getup, Gracie? The
First Fecking Lady?

This was a year ago, several days before Frances Magorian died easily in her sleep. Having drunk one of her potions. The brill thing about them, they were full of everything you already had in the house. That same day she'd said to Grace, Remember me in the same color green, Grace? That dress I usetuh wore to the club?

Frances Magorian hadn't wanted to be forgotten. It was the terrific plight of women who wanted to be remembered, to shack up with men who needed to forget it all.

In a way Grace had felt she could not be free until after Frances was gone. In terms of finding love. After all, think of what she had done to her mother. Yes, of course she'd been groomed for the raping, but hadn't she been complicit? Wasn't it, in the end, also a rape against her mother? She said as much once to a therapist. The therapist, newfangled, was aghast. She had short, gray hair and did not go in for nuance.

She clicked again through his pictures, admiring the JFK jaw, the Irish-American skin that would soon sag but for now still looked lovely on ski trails.

—Why won't you write to me? she whispered.

She put on some Debussy, decanted the claret, and trimmed the artichokes. She floated around the kitchen, selecting the River Cafe olive oil from the suspended shelving, and the coarse Korean gray sea salt from the lit spice display in the wall. You couldn't see the speakers, but the music felt like it was coming from inside your own ears. She'd shown her mother pictures of the Bridgehampton kitchen on her cell. I don't go in for that modernist shite, said the old lady, turning her face away without fully registering the image.

While the artichokes were roasting in the royal-blue La Cornue, Grace cut up a link of wild boar salami and rang Talia on speakerphone. She told her about the man from Venus, the empty email.

Talia was from Pittsburgh by way of Israel, but really she was from nowhere.

—Fuck it, Grace, who cares. You're fucking fifty; you can't afford to play these games. Just write again. What's the name of that site? How's it I haven't heard of it?

—It's invitation only. You have to be invited.

—So fuckin invite me.

—You have to be vetted, Grace said.

—So fuckin invite me, then fuckin vet me already. I think I just had my last period.

Grace pictured Talia in her apartment, a fifth-floor walk-up in China-town, with the racket of the city and the steam of the prawns from the restaurant below. She was in a garnet negligee probably, and perfumed.

—Yeah, I have to uh. I have to be a member for a certain interim, and then.

—You fuckin keeping the keys to the kingdom from me, you ragged cunt?

Grace found Talia mysterious. She did not seem to want any-thing; she just enjoyed the feeling of wanting. They were friends because they were both middle-aged and single. Divorced women did not go near women like Grace and Talia. The fifty-plus never-marrieds were zombies, who ate foul cheese and smelled of crying.

While Talia rattled on about a recent Tinder date—a sixty-something who got drunk, berated a bus girl, and confessed how sad it made him that he no longer cared if a woman was hot; they could have hairy moles on their lips, he just wanted to fuck something that sprung back at him—Grace opened her laptop, logged in to Venus, and wrote to DigLitt: *Are you still out there, love o' my life?* Then she deleted that, and wrote, *Please, I need a sign.* She deleted that, as well.

—Life doesn't end till you wannitu, Frances Magorian said to Grace Magorian as the latter held her glossy blue child to her breast.

—People go when they wannu. Same went for your da.

Was it irrational, Grace thought, to have become so incapacitated because someone she didn't know, never met, had ghosted her?

She sat for a spell in Thing One's hinoki wood soaking tub. The water was scalding and the eucalyptus oil smelled, pleasingly, of poison. But she had never been able to stand a bath. Just sitting there. It seemed so sloppy. She climbed out, her heart racing from the heat of the water. Her hands still dripping, she reached for her phone. An email from *Country Living*. *17 Explosive desserts for the Fourth of July.* Nothing more.

No, it couldn't be. Clearly there was a mail-carrying issue with this stupid, hipster site. Like everything created by millennials, Grace thought, it was beautiful but empty.

It took several minutes, but she found a contact number for Venus. A girl answered, who most definitely had cobalt fingernails. Grace explained the situation, the mostly blank email, the soundlessness that followed. The girl, named Jo, asked for Grace's handle, and for the one belonging to the man she loved. For several minutes there was silence at the other end, and Grace could feel the girl's eyes on her profile, this Cujo who knew nothing, thinking, Yeah, right, this man wrote to you, you old hag. Looking at both their profiles and thinking, Get real, lady.

When her voice returned to the line, Jo told Grace there had been no outages on their end and there was nothing they could do. If somebody didn't write you back, it was recommended that you move on as quickly as possible.

—Then whytha fuck did you ask for our frickin handles!

—I'm sorry, ma'am, the girl said. A voice had never sounded farther away.

Within minutes Grace was naked astride the mahogany captain's chair in Thing Two's office, furiously toggling between windows on her laptop. She searched DigLitt's profile for phrases and places she might string together, to figure out his real name. She did not look for him on Facebook, because his *World at Large* section called social media "an extant place for those who don't think the bad things will happen to them, who think the good are due to them, and want you to know about every Miami vacation."

She spent four hours sleuthing. It was feverish. She didn't realize the time going by. The only time she'd ever felt such a divine slippage of time was at a school dance the year before she became intimate with George. She'd danced most of the night with a boy named Bri'an, who seemed too good for her but did not act it. He wore a plaid blazer, and his skin was attractively acne scarred.

For all her intelligent effort, googling Africa and Brazil and architecture and all the clues in his profile, she could not turn up a LinkedIn or anything. Nothing at all!

She took a pill from Thing One's medicine cabinet. It was a pink oval, like the beginning of a woman. At first she meant only to hold it for another date. She had a storehouse in the studio, of pills and gold bits and bobs she'd been squirreling from the Hoppas these many years. She thought how much easier it would have been for her mother, to have such pretty little pills, instead of the potion of a poor woman, the bleachy rubbish kept under the sink. She placed the pill under her tongue. It felt so small, like it wouldn't do anything at all. So there she placed another.

As the sun set, Grace Magorian began to feel feral. The many years of aloneness piled up inside her like indigestion. She didn't know where the housekeeper was, the landscaper. If anyone was home, alive, in that great breathless house. Naked, she ate the leftover artichokes over the kitchen sink, the army-colored juices streaming down her chin and neck, onto her medium, freckled rack. Then she floated outside, still naked. The backyard was a solitary rectangle of prim lawn encased by privet hedges. There was a pool, of course, as lonely as could be, and two Adirondack chairs gazing into the emerald hinterlands. She took her laptop by the edge of the water, and lay out beside it, feeling the elegant stone against her skin.

She set up a new email; then she invited the new email to Venus. She knew exactly what she wanted and found a series of images, easily, on Facebook. Mary Katherine, was, of course, a few years older than Grace's daughter would have been. But it was close enough.

Grace was tired by then, her eyes warped by the squiggles of text, so she wrote a meager little *About Me* section. She named some movies an eejit might like, said she lived in Fort Greene, enjoyed temperate weather, and the skin of an old book. Grace deleted the last bit, and replaced it with something about art galleries and air travel, called herself Toni, and clicked Save. Then, feeling free, light, shaved of those twenty-plus extra years, she found DigLitt again, his eyes shining coldly in the photograph on the ski run, which he had newly made his main image, meaning he'd been online since she'd written him last.

She moved her head back and forth, to feel the blood whoosh around. Then Grace had Toni tell DigLitt he was *The One*.

Behind the hedges there was a noise. Larger than a rustling. Grace froze. Talia had wanted to come down. She always wanted to come down, drink the booze of rich people and talk about herself. Some-times Talia did impulsive things, but she would have written first.

—Talia? Grace said. No sound returned.

In what felt like an act of self-preservation, Grace got into the pool. It was cold. Even in the heat of summer. Another derivative of Thing Two's penny-pinching.

There was another, louder noise, this one a nagging thump, a human head dropped from a park bench onto grass.

—Hello?

It's him, Grace thought, it's him. Come for me. The way George came, the prefatory night in her room, when Grace figured it was what God sent for her, what He knew she needed—not another fa-ther or a childish lover, but some glorious, steadfast in-between. I am ready, Grace thought, to be swallowed by love!

She'd told Talia on the phone, You don't understand, this man's profile. It is enchanting. He is perfect. Kind and funny and loves all the right books and films. There is a picture of him, for fuck's sake, stirring a huge pot of crayfish with a crescent of Mongolian babes at his knee.

Talia said, Sounds like a regular asshole to me.

Another noise in the brush, this one fantastically loud. And fol-lowed by a whimper, not human, but nor did it sound like it came from an animal, though it must have. It must have been a deer come to die in the brush. Hit by a Range Rover on the Old Montauk Highway, struggled to this private square of land to go tenderly into the night.

Grace Magorian was neither sad, nor afraid. She did not pity, or require any in return.

In the thicket the noise persisted for a minute or less, and then stopped, the way a metronome stops. When the vibrations persist. Grace imagined cool, soft blood, like a quality egg yolk sitting around.

She checked her Toni Magorian email account for what she knew would be there. Her fingertips dripped cool water between the flat keys. She felt young in the pool, as young as she had been before she turned old.

She blacked out maybe, and when she blacked back in, she looked again at her screen. The eyes of the love of her life were startling, truly.

His eyes did not betray him. But Grace knew now, where the good people were. She had always known, of course, that whereas old women for the most part grew into their age gracefully, abandoned the frissons of youth, old men more firmly clawed into the bedrock of their power, their money. If they had none, they hated the world. Hipsters. Bitcoin. If they had plenty, they were afraid of everyone trying to steal it. If they had a stepdaughter, then that was the only time they were afraid of women.

She dipped her head beneath the surface of the water. Her scalp went aqua cold. Down under she couldn't hear anything at all; the whole nut of her was senseless as a toenail. She opened her eyes and realized she had never opened her eyes underwater in the dark, not once in her whole life. There was so much to see. Grace saw the thumbs of her father, the boundaries of his laugh, the great vineyard of his chest. She saw the dance with the young man in the old barn the night that went by too quickly. She saw in the deepest layer of water the bite-blue lips of her child, a young woman for whom all the boys would have gone crazy. All the barn dances, the nights in green dresses. At last, in the hoofing beat of the water, she heard her mother. Stop waiting on 'em, Gracie. Stop looking for them. And then she heard the old lady laugh, as much as someone could hear someone laugh underwater.

Meanwhile the water turned darker and warmer and sweeter. Up above the surface the night changed its clothes. Somewhere someplace forgettable—Philadelphia—a pretty girl played Debussy for an auditorium of throat clearers, having only learned, thus far, to wait for the clap. The music filled the room, stretched itself out to every corner. The music rose to the ceiling and pressed heavily against the doors and dispersed into the thin night, it poured out of speakers in rich kitchens and poor, and all the way down beneath the water it dripped out of those Diluvio ultrasonic speakers that glowed like fucking aliens. So that Grace heard the music loud and clear.

—Yes, ma'am, said Grace Magorian. The best man in the world does not exist. But the best woman. That is me. I am the one you are looking for.

AIR
SUPPLY

WHEN I WAS EIGHTEEN I TOOK A TRIP WITH MY FRIEND SARA TO Puerto Rico. Sara was—and still is—prettier than me, in a slutty 1990s kind of way. Then, as now, she had very straight tan hair. We booked the trip from one of those ads in the newspaper, $299 all-inclusive resort and transfers from El San Juan Hotel & Casino. That was the way people used to book vacations. Or anyway, people like us. Young women from middle-class families.

We both had boyfriends. Hers was an older stock analyst who left his wife for her. Mine was an older goalie coach from Scotland who drank Canadian Club and Coke. At the time, I thought that was debonair.

Neither of us loved our boyfriends. Sara always thought James was cheating on her and vice versa. I didn't worry about my goalie coach cheating. Matter-of-factly he told me he never drank too much outside my presence, because when people drank too much, they did things they regretted. We had only been dating four months, but he acted like it was four years. He was like a woman that way.

Sara's father was driving us to the airport. He was a priest or a deacon, whichever you can be while also having sex with women.

The goalie coach—Mo—dropped me off at Sara's. He made a big show of kissing me goodbye, deep French kissing. He even had flowers. When I got into Sara's father's car, she was peeved. She didn't talk to me for the whole ride and her father asked us the sort of chalky, general questions whose answers a father should already know. Later she told me it was weird that I made out with my boyfriend in front of her father. Because her father was a man of God. I didn't know what to say. I hadn't wanted to make out with Mo, for one, and secondly, when my own father died a few months prior, Sara's father had been like a piece of wood. I'd been hoping for something spiritual to come from him. Instead he approached me a little too amiably, shrugging his shoulders it seemed, and said something like, Time heals all wounds. So I didn't feel badly about making out in front of him.

At the airport bar we ordered drinks at three in the afternoon. Our legs were thin and tan. We were compact, like jockeys. I'd already known tremendous heartbreak and grief, but I would never again be that free, small and effortless.

—It's two for one margaritas, Sara said when I opted for a Bloody Mary on our second round.

—I don't feel like another margarita, I said. The words *feel like*, on my mouth, tasted fine then. In the future, in college and the small years that followed, I would know girls of tremendous wealth, who, even as they scrounged around for dollars to buy a dime bag of weed, had parents in colonials who could sweep them out of bad relationships, evenings. I'd once watched Sara's mother cook a box of Potato Buds after finding not just a cockroach but a small colony of eggs gestating at the top. The church paid for their living expenses, but the church didn't have much.

She clucked her tongue at me, seriously. And quickly forgave me for being an asshole.

━━━━━━━━

It's funny to think about it now, but boys were always looking at us. I mean, every single boy or man we passed. Teenager, married man, old man, whatever. If I weren't enough or Sara wasn't enough to turn a head, then both of us together surely were. These days, I have to be wearing makeup and my hair needs to be straight, or my clothes need to be somewhat suggestive. I guess any kind of a heel will do it, still, but back then all I had to do was breathe air.

When we landed in Puerto Rico, it was nuts. Puerto Rican men, plus men on vacation in general, were even worse than regular men back home in New Jersey. They stared at us. Those long stares, top to bottom, taking a whole person in. Now the world is different, but back then we didn't think about it. If anything, we measured it. We each tried to figure out who was getting more looks. Sara had straight hair and very easy features. You didn't have to stare at her for too long to determine she was pretty. It was a foregone conclusion. I tried to help people out by doing sexual things, lassoing the straw of a drink with my tongue, cocking my neck and body. Nothing worried me more than someone having to calculate my worth, and my having to watch them do it.

On the way to the resort we drove past a lot of poverty. A little boy held a spear and chased a chicken. There were stray dogs everywhere with greasy whiskers. Nobody was combed. The houses were aqua and pink and dirty and browned jungle plants covered windows that had no glass panes. It seemed like every single mother had more than four bare-chested children. We saw so many mothers. I remember thinking each of them was stronger than my own, who didn't know how to write a check or drive a car, who didn't know how to be a parent now that my father was gone. She wanted me to be her husband. I said that to Sara on the drive. She was looking out her window and touching her hair.

—She's just scared, Sara said.

I wanted to hit her, because she never shone that grace on me. She also never worried. I mean it; I never once saw her worry. You could say we were young, but even a decade later when her mother had to get both breasts lopped off Sara said she had faith that everything would go as it should. I took that to mean she didn't love her parents as deeply as I loved mine. Or as much as I'd loved my father, in any case, who'd been better than hers. Who'd been more of a man of God, even though he cursed and smoked and sped on the highway up until the day he died on one.

———

The first night we went to the casino in our hotel right after dinner. I wore a one-shouldered red dress that was tight around my hips and rear and Sara wore a light-blue terry halter dress. Back then, I think I had the better body. My butt and legs were more exciting. But Sara was a little taller and her neck was a little longer, so at first glance it seemed she had the better body. Now she definitely does. She lost a lot of weight after she had her baby. I didn't. But it was easier for her. She was barely eating.

Sara didn't gamble, so I played blackjack at a ten-dollar table and she stood behind me, like my girlfriend. She hated the idea of gambling, of wasting money on anything, but she loved that we were getting free drinks from the casino bar. She drank vodka cranberries with lime. I drank Bloody Marys even though it was nighttime. We got very drunk, though in retrospect that first night was the tamest. We went to our room and changed. I put on a silky bustier with a cherry print and a long swinging skirt. We splashed around in a fountain in the hotel lobby. Nobody told us to stop. It was only me who splashed around, actually, and she took a picture of me. I still have the picture. I can't believe I ever worried about how I looked back then. In the picture I'm supertan and my hair is very black against my warm skin and I'm incredibly thin but also curvy. When I look at that picture, I feel I am looking at the most beautiful girl.

We danced at a bar on the beach and every guy in the place came up to us. Bought us blue drinks or white ones. I put cigarettes out into bottles of Corona. Sara and I made out with each other because that was something we occasionally did. I gently held Sara's scalp in my hands. I knew what to do to make men crazy like that. Her lips were very soft, I'll never forget that, but I never thought much about her in those moments. I was too busy thinking about what it looked like, from the outside.

Sara got the kind of drunk she always got. Her body swayed and her eyes grew small and unreliable. I seldom got drunk like that. I became triumphant and then sick. But Sara could sway for hours, like a weak boat in the ocean. For the last eighth of the evening we'd been talking to two boys from Cincinnati. I'd never met anyone from Cincinnati and still to this day haven't met another. It's one of the only places in the country I haven't driven through. I'm sure Sara has been there. She works for a cancer foundation and their conferences are held in places like that.

The boys were a little older than us, juniors or seniors in college. One of them was much better looking than the other. Sara always liked whichever guy was more outgoing. I guess I did, too. But I placed a higher value on attractiveness than she did. The better-looking one liked Sara better. Or she was drunker. I don't know. But I bowed out at some point. I think about how many tiny competitions I've engaged in over the years, with Sara and other friends who followed. It all feels like a waste of time and yet, if I were back there again, knowing what I know now, I don't think I'd do it any differently. I think I'd still wink at a boy behind my best friend's back.

The good-looking one came back to our room with us. He and Sara held hands and I walked ahead of them with the room key. I was tired and bored and thought how at least back at home I could talk to Mo about the poetry of song lyrics.

The boy from Cincinnati gave Sara oral sex in her bed. I fell asleep to the sound of lapping noises. When we were in middle school, Sara was one of the only girls with a steady boyfriend. He was Chilean and very good-looking and I used to watch them inside the vestibule after school, making out slow and soft. I was jealous; Sara and I were not yet friends and I had never been kissed. I am still jealous, all these years later, even after she told me that boy's hands used to always smell of penis. That once she even asked him if he had just touched his penis and he admitted that he had. I am still jealous, even after all the rest.

When we woke up the guy was gone and Sara's dress was bunched up around her waist like a silly belt. I'd forgotten to call my mother the night before and Sara had forgotten to call her boyfriend, so we spent the whole morning drinking orange juice in the Jacuzzi tub by one of the many pools, calming the people back home and being somewhat angry at each other, because it was a cloudy day and we had headaches.

By the afternoon we had fully recovered. We ate ceviche for lunch and I insisted on driving to the Old City that night. On the way we had to look for a pharmacy because Sara had bad heartburn. It was the only time I'd ever seen her complain of a physical ailment. In the future I would become something of a hypochondriac and Sara would laugh at me, at the notion of a young, healthy person contracting a rare and terrible disease.

Sara didn't help me look. Our relationship, especially then, was like that of a 1950s couple. I was the man and she was the housewife. She was quiet and always looking out of windows. She expected me to bring the fun to her, to decide where we would eat and how we would get home. I was used to the role. It was the relationship my parents had, and the one my mother now wanted to re-create with me.

—It's really bad, she said, pressing a hand to her chest as we pulled into the central business district of Old San Juan. Did you see any pharmacies?

—Yes, I said, but I didn't stop.

—Huh? Why?

I parked the car in what seemed to be the most amazing spot. Right in front of the statue of San Cristóbal. We could see the ocean and the whole city beneath us. It was dusk, very different from back home. There were so many little stars they looked like chicken feed in the sky. It was easier that my father was dead, there in Puerto Rico, than home in New Jersey. I felt sorry for my mother, but in a more removed sense than usual.

Sara and I were both wearing heels. We walked uneasily down the cobblestone roads. It was humid and the air was fragrant with the smell of flowers and sweat and food. Over some of the hillier parts, Sara took hold of my hand, even though I was wearing taller heels.

We both had no idea where the night would go, how south it would go, how freakishly memorable.

I picked out a lively gastrobar with lime-green chairs. Sara's only requirement for dining was that the restaurant had outdoor seating and carafes of inexpensive house wine. To this day she is like that, even with sushi restaurants. My husband and I only eat at places with a certain number of five-star reviews. Atmosphere is eschewed in favor of quality of food, but back then Sara and I only wanted pergolas, greenery, tuna tartare served on palm leaves.

I smoked cigarettes in between courses. Our waiter and our busboy fancied us both. Probably me more. I was more engaged with service staff. I spoke Spanish decently. Sara wasn't hampered by not knowing the language. Her smile was like a passport. She was confident and perennially happy, even with the heartburn. Anyway, we did find a *farmacia* after all, right before dinner. I placed three Spanish-language Tums on her tongue. I went through the roll to find the pink ones.

I wanted to order the *molletes criollos*, but Sara wouldn't have liked it. She hated fried, fatty things, probably because of the way she grew up. She liked raw fish, clean, melony flavors. Fruit salads. I ordered a grouper cured with citrus served on a bed of scissored jicama.

—Yum, she said, when the plate arrived. We drank so much wine, our waiter kept refilling our glasses. We laughed a lot. I remember the temperature of my skin, like a tomato all day in the sun. My upper lip was raw with sunburn. I'd thought it would take a lot to not feel my loss, as wide and sharp as though I'd been bitten by a tiger, but it turned out that feeling young and pretty and free in Puerto Rico did the trick.

—I want to break up with James, she said. She always said that, but on this night it seemed more probable.

—Are you sure? I asked.

—It's not going anywhere. I don't like that he does so much coke.

—You do coke.

—Yeah, but only because of him. I want to be with someone who wouldn't let me do coke.

—Did you guys make up from last night? I asked. That was my way of making up with Sara. We both knew it. It was a question I should have asked hours ago, when she got off the phone with him.

—I don't know. He's going to Robby's bachelor party next weekend. I feel like I need to break up with him before that. I want to be free.

—You're kind of free, I said, referring to the night before, the boy in her bed. She smiled.

—I mean free not to worry about what he's doing.

—Right, I said.

Her relationship with James would go on for several more feckless years. We would have hundreds of conversations like that one, and nothing would ever change. They would have wild fights. One night James would punch a hole in a motel room door to get to her, like *The Shining*. One night, after another friend's wedding, he would call Sara things like *whore* and *white trash* as I drove them back to his apartment. One night, shortly after the funeral of my mother, Sara would introduce me to a boy she thought would take my mind off this fresh, new death, and James would think she was trying to sleep with the boy she was fixing me up with. I would think the same. But still, their relationship persisted, right up until the day it ended, without fanfare, rather bloodlessly. She'd met someone new, someone who also did coke, but knew it was bad. The new man called cocaine Bad guy, and she laughed telling me about this. I would think back to her relationship with James, and to what it meant in relation to our own friendship. It had always been such a looming thing. There had ever been something comforting about its big, graceless presence. And something sad about its end.

Right after we finished our entrees was when the night turned. Not into something terrible, even though then it did feel terrible. Now it's probably one of the nicest memories I have.

We noticed, for the first time, a group of men sitting nearby. There were five of them, two older men in their fifties, and three younger ones in their twenties. On their table was a pitcher of margaritas, several kinds of mixed drinks, shiny Tecates, plus a jeroboam of Grey Goose and a carafe of cranberry juice. Half of them were smoking. The young ones were vaguely good-looking, with interesting haircuts. The older ones were thick gutted, spiky haired. They were interesting in a wealthy-seeming way. The table as a whole was raucous. I took a cigarette from my mother's antique silver holder. I heard the snap of a Zippo before I saw the light.

—Ladies, ladies, said one of the younger ones. Rotund face, inky hair and brows. His breath smelled like he needed to floss. I'll never forget it. What is it about men with bad breath that makes me feel raped? I would ask Sara later. She would scrunch her eyes and shake her head at me, like I was nuts. I didn't remind her of her boyfriend with the penis hands. She wouldn't have made the connection.

—Are you guys famous? I said.

—What tipped you off? said one of the two older men. British accent, grin like a squiggly line, accordion neck. To this day, I don't know what he meant by that. By that same logic, I don't know what made me think they were famous.

Sara sipped on her margarita straw, blinking at them like a girl deer.

They told us who they were. A pop-rock band, started by the two older ones back in the late seventies. I'd heard of the name. I knew my older brother would know them. What I didn't know then, what I would forget to look up for many years, was that it was not so much a band but a duo, that the younger ones were not part of the band, but only backup. Just because they could say they were in the band, it didn't mean anything. I didn't know that then. So I flirted with the younger ones. Sara had never heard of them at all, but somehow she was like a heat sensor for relevance. She went to sit beside Graham, the old Brit with the spiky hair and the beige teeth.

We got drunk, shots and sangria. Before the group disbanded, we took a photograph I still have. Jan and the members of the band seated or standing by the bar. Me like a kayak they were carrying at their sides. That and the picture of me in the fountain are the only two pictures I have of Puerto Rico. This was the time before cell phones.

I don't know exactly how the next thing happened. I was drunk. I was tired of making sure a woman was all right. But I let Sara leave with Graham. It was nuts that she did that. She wasn't scared of anything, but she also somehow, like I've described, had this great trust at the right times. I am not jealous of that but admiring. Every time I am faced with the tiniest adversity, I think of Sara, how I (almost always) wish I were her and not me.

The first thing that happened was the bandmates were walking us to our car; we were going to follow them to their swanky hotel for nightcaps. But I'd forgotten where our rental was parked. I stopped a passing local and asked in Spanish, Excuse me, where is the statue of San Cristóbal?

He cocked his head at me. He looked at our whole group. He

laughed cruelly. There are *many* statues of San Cristóbal, he said, and walked away.

—Oh, you didn't know that? Sara said to me. The members of the band laughed. Miss Smarty-Pants, she said, made a mistake.

It was right that I was brought to my knees. But I was still enraged. I said I would find the car by myself and meet them at the hotel. The young inky-haired one said he would help me. I watched Sara walk off, clopping like a pony, on Graham's arm. I had the thought that I would never see her again.

I took my heels off and the boy—Jake—carried them. My memory is fuzzy for this part. I was the drunkest then, and the happiest. We went into shallow tequila bars, took shots. Colored fiesta lights hung from almost every entrance. My throat burned in a way that made me feel alive. These days, I never take shots. I pronounce them immature before an evening even gets started.

—My father died, I said to Jake, when I felt he was about to kiss me.

—Mine too, he said.

Back home whenever Mo felt me slipping away he would say he missed his da. He didn't know I had a magical power, being that I could tell when people didn't miss their dead.

When Jake did this same thing, I jumped and hung and swung from the lunglike cord of a banyan tree.

—Whoa! he said, putting his arms out like he needed to catch me. I swung mightily back and forth, using my legs like levers, like I was on a swing. I don't remember falling, but I must have at some point, from a banyan tree later in the evening. There were so many. I know I fell because my head hurt like hell in one spot the whole next day. Back then I didn't think anything of it. These days, I'd be getting an MRI.

I don't know how many bars we stopped in. He tried to kiss me several more times. His breath was truly terrible. He was American, trying to look British. He acted decades younger than Mo and yet they were equally boyish in their manhood. My father had never been a boy. My uncle confirmed this. My father was a man even at eleven, when he twisted a rabid dog's neck in his hands, killing it instantly as it was lunging after a little neighbor girl. He was a man at twenty-one when, studying medicine abroad, he'd sent gold chains home from Italy, with a note informing his mother that 18-karat gold was less expensive in Italy. He was a man all the days of my life, except, if I'm being clinical, on the day he got himself killed speeding on a highway. Only a boy lets himself get killed that way.

You think you know so much about men, Sara had said to me earlier that day, when we were still raw and hungover. The Jacuzzi water was tepid. A skin of gray froth had collected at the corners. These days, I don't go in Jacuzzis recklessly. I only go at expensive hotels where the people are sure to be cleaner than me.

—I do, I said, thinking of my father versus her father at the top of a building somewhere.

—You are a know-it-all, she said. She had a way of rolling her eyes that made me feel instantly insecure, even when her words did precisely the opposite. Once I'd corrected her pronunciation of the word *mischievous. Miss*-chee-vee-*ous*, she said. I laughed at her. In some weird part of me, I was angry at her for saying the word like that.

At some point in the streets of San Juan, in the purple-green light of a certain bar, I was truly worried I wouldn't see Sara again. I felt idiotic for correcting her pronunciation. She was so pretty that she wouldn't need to pronounce words correctly. Maybe that's what had angered me so.

Magically then, I looked up a hill and remembered that was where the car was, just beyond a church.

—I was hoping we would never find it, Jake said, in a way he must have thought was romantic. I've been repulsed many times since, but that was one of the worst instances.

Jake said he would drive. No, I said, the rental car is in my name.

I'd mentioned I wanted to see the rainforest. He said there was an entrance we could go to. An after-hours entrance that he knew about.

—I have to get my friend, I said.

—She's fine.

Men who want to fuck are always very sure of everyone who is fine. I'm sure most times they are right. I have never wanted to fuck more than I have wanted to make sure someone is fine. I'm absolutely sure Sara is the opposite.

—Where are you all staying?

—Uh. The Condado.

—Is that where Graham is?

He was touching a bracelet on my wrist. I repeated the question.

—I think he's at the St. Regis.

—They're not footing your bill?

—They are, Jake said, confused, then angry.

—Do you know how to get there?

—Nope, he said. I wanted to hit him in his dirty mouth. I have never respected men who don't know direction. The reason I had agreed to come with Sara on this vacation, to Puerto Rico in particular, was because years ago I had come here with my parents. I'd walked for an hour on the beach alone, at thirteen, in a black two-piece with technicolor butterflies on it. A man in his forties told me I was beautiful, asked me where I was from. I didn't tell my parents. I wasn't yet aware of pedophiles. I was disturbed enough to not tell my parents anything. One day during that vacation we were driving across the island and we hit a giant traffic jam. The kind that never happened back home. My father was at the tail end of it, and when he saw the pileup he swore and began driving backwards. Quickly, others began to follow his lead, driving backwards to the most recent exit. An entire highway of people driving backwards. I would never forget it.

That night with the boy in my car, I tried to summon my father's confidence. There was no GPS back then; I can't believe I survived. So much of life is like that. How did we get by? we think. And yet when we look back on the past, mostly we see happiness.

And thank God, also, we didn't have cell phones. I could not have handled James calling me and calling me while I was looking for Sara. I would have to tell him she was dead. He would kill me.

Finally, I don't know how, perhaps it was the will of my father, we found the hotel. I found the hotel. It was much lovelier than ours, very modern and well-appointed. At the lobby I asked for Graham's room. He was not staying under a different name because he was not that famous. At this point I lost Jake. To this day I have no idea where he went. He was probably in the lobby bar, trying to pick up something that moved.

I walked up to Graham's room and knocked. Twice. Three times. Nothing. I began to tremble. I pictured Sara in there, raped and aspirating on her own vomit. I began to pound on the door.

He opened the door wearing a dressing gown. This half-dead fifty-something.

—Where's Sara?

—What?

—My best friend!

How silly of me, I think now. But I can still remember the pulsing in my veins at the time. Perhaps that was where the love lived, in tiny inaccessible veins that only coursed when they needed to. By contrast, Sara loved things with a certain freedom I didn't have the emotional intelligence to comprehend.

Graham yawned and pushed the door all the way open.

—She's fine, he said. She's sleeping.

I walked up to the bed. The tile floors of the islands have always depressed me. They are cold and cheap, made to withstand moisture. You can clean bugs easily from the corners.

—Sara! I said. I touched her. She was still in her dress.

—Hey, she said, smiling sleepily. She was always happy; she never minded being woken.

—We have to go.

—Mmm, I'm cozy.

—We have to go.

—I want to sleep here. Sleep with me, she said, opening the covers up for me. I carried her out of the room, in my arms like a baby. Graham held the door for us. He kissed Sara on the nose while she was in my arms. It was an absolutely ludicrous situation. But what happened next is where the night got truly dark.

We were both drunk. Sara, of course, was drunker. I was more so exhausted. Drunk didn't last on me. I was driving through the streets, trying to find our hotel. Sara fell asleep, or maybe I'd carried her to the car and strapped her in while she slept. But we were both out of it until I hit a bump, something so huge that the car became airborne for a moment. Sara startled, angry.

—What the hell!

—Are you fucking kidding me, I said.

—Watch how you're driving!

I wanted to kill her, but there wasn't enough time. That bump had been like a descent into another world. Suddenly we were on a residential street. Full of cars, some with smashed windows. We saw roosters, or we heard them first.

Later I would learn that cockfighting was something like Puerto Rico's national sport. It was legal but only in sanctioned arenas. A lot of fights went on underground to avoid the taxes and fees the government had instituted. This one, that we had unwittingly stumbled upon, was definitely underground. Plus it was late at night, outside in the middle of an abandoned park.

A big man in a leather vest approached our car, banged a shotgun against my window.

Sara screamed.

I was angry at her for being OK with my father's death, for thinking I should be over it and available only for my mother, but now here being scared at a shotgun in the window.

I rolled down my window.

—Turista? the man bellowed into the crack of the window.

—Get us out of here! Sara screamed.

I was fearless. I had nothing left to lose. My mother had not even yet been diagnosed. I actually had a lot left to lose, but I was as stupid as Sara. We were stupid, pretty girls.

—Ella, si, I said pointing to Sara. Pero yo, no. *Yo* soy una viajera.

At first his gun moved and I peed a hot squirt into my underwear. Then he laughed.

—Ven y mira el espectáculo, he said. Five *dolares* only.

I parked the car. Sara stopped freaking out and we walked through a makeshift entrance demarcated by two wooden poles in the ground. We passed a pudgy boy a ten-dollar bill and he seemed shocked.

On the other side was a brightly lit old baseball field. Seating was made up of rustic wooden benches, church pews, dusty folding chairs. In the center was a ring that looked like an old aboveground pool. It was filled with packed sand atop which two roosters were flapping around at each other. Some men leaned their bodies over the edge of the pit, screaming at the animals like they could understand. The roosters pecked at each other's faces. They could have just as easily been playing and not engaging in some blood sport. After we got home we would talk about it, the horror of it, but in the middle of it, it was slow-moving, boring even. Perhaps Sara felt differently, but I don't think so. We were simply cognizant we were doing something interesting. Something that would read as more interesting later, like all things. The best part of the fight was that none of the men were looking at us, and it was mostly men in the arena. Some women in tight black pants, some in short shorts, some little girls with long lustrous hair. But mostly men who wanted nothing to do with us. They were all shouting at the ring, waving their own hands like troubled wings.

I would also learn later that caring for the roosters, the fighters, before and after each fight, was its own occupation. There was someone to spray the battered birds with a solution of hydrogen peroxide and water. Someone to put antibiotic drops in their bloodshot eyes. It was a big operation. Anyway, maybe someone would have hit on us during an intermission, but we left before the fight ended.

Sara nudged me, said, Take me home, so I did. In the car she told me she had never been more scared.

Our night ended at a taco joint on the highway, where I finally stopped to ask for directions. We ordered tacos. I ordered them for us. The meat was crumbly. The spices were old tasting. I watched Sara eat and swallow. I was happy she was eating. Happy she was hungry. I felt the night was my fault. That it would live in her mind as a bad memory because of me. I hated myself, even though I always said I loved myself. I was impressed with myself. My father loved me so much. But I didn't pick up the phone the day he called before he got in the car. Why? I don't know. I guess I wasn't worried yet then. I was as free as Sara would always be.

In the taco joint we were stared at by everyone. That's easy, though. Late at night any bare-legged girl eating food in a dingy place might as well be screaming, Fuck me, into a megaphone. I had mascara under my eyes, and there was Sara, big lipped, swaying. All the men in there were looking at us like we were the most beautiful girls in the world.

When we got back from Puerto Rico, we needed a certain amount of time. A week or so, apart from each other. And then it was back to normal. We were inseparable for a time. We attended the same college briefly, after I left my better one to be closer to a boy I was seeing.

Throughout our life, Sara would always keep in touch. She always wanted me to stay with her, always wanted to see me. There wasn't a day after Puerto Rico that she didn't want to see me. She made lots of other friends, but I was always her favorite. I made some friends who didn't mispronounce words, who didn't book cheap, impulsive vacations. I would always love Sara best, but I wouldn't always need to see her the way she needed to see me.

———

In the further future, one or both of us would try Cannabis Oil, Transcendental Meditation. One man, while underneath her, would tell her she had concave little tits. And she would stop fucking him, midair, just like that, like an acrobat.

We would turn twenty-four and twenty-six and thirty. We would be leaving an acquaintance's funeral—heroin, Cape Cod—and the dead boy's father would turn to look at us, our rears.

—We've still got it, Sara would say to me. I laughed out loud, because I'd been thinking the very same thing.

In the further, further future, the boyfriend, James, became hip, founded a very lucrative business. Sara showed me his business card. It said, *Are you an alcoholic? Yes? We can help. 14/7 Liquor Delivery.*

Even though he got wealthy and bought a sauna-toned home in Aspen, Sara would never once ask me, Should I have stayed with him? I bet she didn't even ask herself.

I would have a child first. My brother would say I looked doughy shortly after the birth. My husband and I would see a fat couple in a car next to us, with a Beanie Baby on the windshield. He would say, That is us in ten years. I would say, I can read lips and the woman just said to the man, Honey, doesn't that look like us, just last year?

I would call my husband a whale that farts. Sara would fuck her husband more than any friend we knew. She would love my baby, a girl, more than most of our relatives did. She would love her as though we had spent nearly every day together for the past fifteen years, and not only the ones around the holidays.

Sara would continue to clip coupons and look for cheap vacations in the newspaper. I would live beyond my means, child in tow. Every time I broke an egg yolk and threw it out, Sara would be the only thing I would think of.

We would tell the story of the band we met; sometimes people would say, Oh my god, you met *them*! Other times, they wouldn't recognize the name. Or they would pretend to have heard of them. The way Sara did that night.

One day Sara would call to tell me James had died. Holy shit, I said. How? Don't laugh, she said. You're a cruel person. No, I promise I'm not, I said. She told me he'd been in Kazakhstan, competing in a beer-drinking contest wherein the competitor places a clear keg of beer over his head and has to drink it all before he drowns.

—It feels like the only way he would have wanted to go, I said.

Neither of us laughed; a piece of our friendship had died with James. Anyway, there was more important news. Sara had predominantly called to say she was expecting, finally. The last of our friends to get pregnant, though it was widely understood she was the only one fit to be a mother.

In a restaurant shortly after the election of Trump, my husband would scream at Sara, not because Sara voted for him, but because she didn't hate him enough. Sara was still living in our small town. She didn't agree with his policy, she believed gay people should be married, but she said something about the emails. Whatever it was, my husband exploded. Publicly, I took her side. She was pregnant, and I still hated myself for correcting her pronunciation, for not sleeping over her new house. Privately, I took his. Both of them hated me for it. I have always been a coward. That night, she went into labor.

Something bad happened. There was a lack of oxygen. A lack of air because of the cord.

I don't know. Shortly after the child's birth she told me what happened, but either she didn't explain it well or I didn't listen well or a combination of the two. Anyway, there is no point in figuring out the mechanics of something like that. They have adequate medical care. Beyond that, Sara has the kind of faith that doesn't care to get particular with the details. That is her way. I told my husband that. He shook his head, as though I should know more.

For six months everything was fine, but then she called me again. Because of the issue that happened at birth, the lack of air, there would have to be an eight-hour surgery immediately. This week. It would be fine, she said, she had faith. But did I want to come?

My husband and I spent many hours looking on the Internet. The surgery was called precarious, everywhere we looked. It had a fifty-fifty success rate. The opposite of success, in this case, was death. Sara's baby is the finest baby I've ever met. I love his face, his eyes. I never love babies enough. Sometimes I worry I don't love my own enough.

—You only love him like that because of what he's going through, my husband said, because he can be cruel.

—She went into labor that night because you yelled at her, I said. It's all your fault.

———

The day of the surgery, Sara is wearing a tan suit. I don't know why she is wearing a suit. She looks beautiful, as always. She has never degenerated. She has still not got Botox. Her breasts are still flat, but so is her stomach.

I wondered if I should bring books. When my parents, one after the other, perished in a hospital, there was no hope either time. Thus, no books. On my way out the door that morning, my husband rips my paperback of *The Stranger* out of my hand. Not because the situation is hopeless, he says, but because I am.

We are in the waiting room until she asks, Do you want to take a walk? Her husband sits there, watching a Colts game on the small overhead television. If it were me I would not leave the area, but like

I have said, Sara has a certain inalienable faith. Plus she loves taking walks. When we both smoked, she used to love going outside for cigarettes, with me specifically.

I am wearing a torn gray sweatshirt and black yoga pants. I have not lost enough of the baby weight, and my child is nearly three years old. I'm too busy being worried all the time, while Sara puts her energy into working out. Still, I wear makeup today, because looking attractive helps me cope. Anyway, I think, it is not my infant in there. I can be forgiven.

We are walking down the hall. We are very close to each other. I'm wearing sneakers and she's wearing a nude, low heel. She smells like freesias. She has always smelled beautiful, despite the homes she was living in. She hooks her arm into mine. I grasp her hand. I can't remember the last time we walked close, holding each other like this. And then I do. She was holding me like this in Puerto Rico. In her cheap pleather heels.

Right before we enter the cafeteria, we pass by a trio of three doctors in lab coats. Stethoscopes give me a pang, still, make me think of my father. I should have married a physician, I scream at my husband whenever I have a cold.

These doctors, they are young and powerful and attractive, and I can't believe the way it happens, like a cartoon. Their heads turn. All three of them. Maybe it is just at Sara, but my hair is so glossy, I've recently dyed it. Also, I'm wearing makeup, and perhaps in my shirred sweatshirt I remind them of the girl from *Flashdance*. Their eyes grow wide, one of them smiles, and another blushes. Sara and I look at each other, and I hate myself for thinking it, but maybe not as much as she hates herself. In the times that really count, we have always been one and the same woman. So I know what both of us are thinking.

MAID
MARIAN

IN LINE AT THE ALDI, HER PHONE VIBED TWICE. SHE REMOVED IT from her Herschel hip pack, an accessory Harry had claimed to love. Am I too old for it? she'd asked him, the first time she'd worn it in his presence. You will never be old enough, he'd said, kissing the top of her head. And ruffling her hair, or what remained of it.

She opened her email application and there it was: *RE: [The Moorehead Foundation] Noni Lemm. Dear Ms. Lemm, Thank you for your submission to the Moorehead Documentarian Grant. While we lalalala, we regret to inform you that you are not a recipient of the grant this year. Please know that it was an extremely competitive lalalala.*

The second note was from the March of Dimes. She'd donated twenty dollars once, on a fair day of her life, and they kept now coming back for more, and always in her darkest hours.

—Fuck you, she said aloud. Fuck you, and you, and you, and yoo-hoo.

The lady behind Noni was foreign, engaged with a change purse. The cashier before her was multiply pierced and purple lidded. In short, nothing Noni said or did mattered out here. Torrington, Connecticut. Close enough to the *bellezza* of the country, Washington

Depot and Roxbury, the fine towns with the shampooed cows, but far enough that it could not be easily said that she'd moved out there to be closer to Harry. Anyway, Harry's estate on Painter Ridge Road was only a weekend home. Marian, his second wife, kept a horse in a stable down the road, and she liked to ride him on the trails when the leaves burned gold. But her interest had waned in recent years. Marian's sister had purchased a home in Sagaponack and so Harry and Marian had started going there, packing up their old but rich Saab with city treats, cheeses and lemony liqueurs. Marian's sister also had an eighteen-month-old son, huge headed and timorous. Harry disliked beaches and children, so over scones in the city Noni said, Your personal hell, sandy diapers. Harry had smiled, nodded, folded his hands, and surveyed the little café they were in, which reminded Noni of Paris, when he'd been her teacher, when she'd had beet-colored hair that she dyed with hibiscus and wore velvet pants and smoked clove cigarettes. It's not so bad, he'd said. He couldn't know, of course, how a little nothing line like that was a stake in her gut.

Not receiving the Moorehead grant was a blow but not a surprise. Noni had long ago resigned herself to not being one who glittered. She was respected in the community; she held posts in all the right groups and had several visiting professorships, one of which provided on-campus housing, for which she'd thanked the dean profusely, and he'd cut her off like she was a much younger person: Because you're single, because you have no family, it's easy. It's only an apartment. She was respected, but not celebrated. She was a member of the court but by no means a monarch.

Harry, on the other hand, had been a king. One of the few who bridged the chasm between critical acclaim and mainstream relevance. A celebrity, if the field could be said to have them. Plus he had the accoutrements. The pipe, the womanizing. "The Hemingway of poetic documentarians," the *Guardian* had christened him, in a piece for which they'd interviewed Noni.

The reporter, young and attractive, had come to Noni's studio when she'd still lived in the city. Noni brewed oolong and they sat on the floor, against the plump but threadbare Moroccan pillows. The reporter wore mustard stockings and riding boots. She had long legs and knew precisely how to fold them. She asked what the most important thing was that Harry had taught her. The two women gazed for a long while into each other's eyes. Noni took in the angle of her face, the smooth fur of her pink cheek. The reporter's eye, glinting and alluring, with no eyeliner, perhaps a tender scrape of mascara, perhaps nothing at all.

How to build a fire, Noni said, at last, and the reporter took the line down dutifully, and also with ease. Of course, Noni realized, he'd fucked her.

At the time she hadn't thought to care how she'd be presented in the story. She hadn't thought she'd appear much at all. But she should have known. The young reporter had been cruel, in her way. She wrote that Noni was the type to say she loved the smell of old books. That her hair was light brown and unassuming (by which of course she meant *homely*), and the bitch had also said the thing that Noni knew was public record and yet she couldn't believe the way her words had been used. The second time the reporter saw Noni was at a soiree for Harry, during which the faux-intellectual minx had been shadowing him. Noni was holding court with a few lesser-thans, in a corner with some Fernet and twinge. One of them, a man who'd been trying to get in her pants for ages, asked Noni if she and Harry had ever been an item. Simply, she hadn't thought. The reporter had been circulating, swishing her mane, sedately taking notes on her mobile phone.

In the article that came out the next month, the reporter had written that when she, when Noni, publicly used the word *fuck*, as in, *If you mean did we fuck then yes, we fucked, ages ago*, you could divide the room into the half who were charmed and the half who were somewhat repelled. The reporter devoted an entire paragraph to the idea that, to many, a woman Noni's age was rather old to have *fucked*. Mind you, she was not *old*. But she was the type of fifty-six to sixty-four who some people think should always wear turtlenecks, hide their sex, expose only the noblesse of their mortality. The reporter used this notion to contrast with Harry, nearly a decade older than Noni, but swaggering around the room, vivacious, grand, an *objet* all his own.

When the story broke, Noni wrote to Harry right away. *I'm so sorry*, she said. *I didn't know that woman was around me, and. Shit. Marian knew, though, yes?*

A message came through a few minutes later: *She knew, yes. She didn't love to see it in print that way. But she'll calm down.*

After checking out of the Aldi with her grapes and her flaxseed bread, her knobby avocadoes and her frozen salmon portions, Noni stopped by the post office to get her mail. It had been an adjustment, moving to the country from the city. The dirt roads, the Trump voters. Every blue-collar worker with corrugated skin, you couldn't be sure what darkness might lie beneath the tawny exterior. The postmaster general, a round-faced woman named Bernadette, smiled brightly at Noni when she walked in. Noni smiled back. She was blindingly polite but uninviting. She kept to herself even more so in the country than she had in the city. She crossed the chilly room and opened her brass box. It was full, mostly with flyers, trade magazines, the usual waste she would pile in a picnic basket and use to stoke a fire come winter. Then she saw it. A thin business envelope, from a lawyer's office in the city. Inside, a cornflower slip of paper. At first the words didn't make sense, and she merely felt his loss all over again, like a great submerging. Noni was grateful for the solitude in the post office, only herself and Bernadette. She read the words again: a slender paragraph, plus a time, date, and location at which her presence was requested. She clutched the paper to her heart and gasped.

———

It was true that Harry taught her how to build a fire. She'd been twenty-one, in his furnished rental on the Île Saint-Louis. There'd been a blackened fire pit, so cavernous and ill defined it could have been a room all its own. He sat on his armchair in the otherwise bare room and instructed her on how to form a nest. She'd been trembling. Terrified of disappointing him. He was her teacher then, and already a small god. *Think of the fire as something that should not be given a moment of pause. It should be like that in any story you tell. There should never be a moment when the audience can get up to take a piss. You see? You must run them, keep running them, until they die. The same with a fire. All the logs should join, they should all rise up, and the fire should climb and mount until it can't breathe anymore, and begins to descend. You lay the groundwork in the beginning, and you won't have to do anything in the middle. The key is to build the fire that does not need watching. We should be able to lie here all night, and never get up. Now, come here.*

This night, she made a fire. It was only October, but it had been cool throughout the county since Labor Day. She changed from her street clothes into a slip and a boucle sweater. She fed the flames her *Republican-Americans*, that were free in most of the stores and delis of Litchfield County. She was sure nobody read them. They just liked to display the little yellow mailboxes outside their homes. The flames licked the grainy image of a local councilman.

The fireplace in this rented house was in the dining room, which Noni had turned into her editing space. She was a frugal worker. Two screens and a filing cabinet comprised her bay. The fireplace was staid, with a brass grate and a slate floor. The whole house was very workmanlike. In a county full of farms and barns and rusty silos vandalized into artist's studios, Noni's rental was a bare-bones 1920s carriage house, renovated in the eighties and anodyne. There was one large bedroom and a little anteroom that Noni used as storage. The anteroom had a wallpaper border of a stork holding a blue satchel of baby, replicated in perpetuity. Before she rented it, a childless couple had begun to build a nursery. Noni didn't know any further details, only that they'd left before their lease was up, fortuitously for her, who'd decided at the same time not to renew in the city. By then, Harry and Marian had owned the house in Roxbury for a year. Noni had taken the train up three times to visit. He'd pick her up in New Milford, and mostly they would drive around. She loved the roads that dipped down into valleys of farmland, then up past old airplane hangars and little woodsheds full of corn for sale.

The project she was currently working on was called *The Republican-American*—like the paper. She was interviewing people in the county, people like Bernadette, who voted Republican but only thought they knew why.

—Good, Harry said. But what's the goal?

—The goal? What are your goals?

—Noni. You're not *curieux* enough, still. You have good ideas and a brilliant little engine; what is your end game?

Once again, they were seated before a fireplace. This one in his Roxbury home. A converted barn from Stone Arabia, with cypress floors, on seven hilly acres. Marian was in Los Angeles for a film premiere. They hadn't been alone in a house together since Helene, his first wife, had come home early from the symphony—it was a second-string cellist and she hadn't been able to bear it—and found Noni and Harry on the couch, laughing, seated too close.

But Marian was different. She was self-possessed, and also far younger than Helene, and younger than Noni, too. Besides all that, she was thousands of miles away.

Nothing happened that night, nothing if you didn't count the looks they shared, their eyeballs like lasers on each other. It was as though they'd both been acting like their audio were being recorded, but not visual. They talked shop, they talked about old friends, they talked about nothing at all, and yet the whole night was full of thirst. They drank too much Bordeaux. Too much for Noni, anyhow. She fell asleep on the couch. He'd covered her with an antique pink gauze blanket, one of Marian's beauties. Everything the woman owned was over five hundred dollars.

In the morning Harry was even more tender. He'd got up before her, driven to procure lox and bagels and glorious red onions. Coffee, and cream from one of the dairy farms with the splendid Holstein cows. While he was gone, Noni rinsed in the outdoor shower, used Marian's jewel soap that smelled of vacation, used Marian's waffle-knit bathrobe that weighed more than Noni's whole life.

She emerged to find a breakfast laid out by the slate pool. Harry swimming naked, this great beast with thatches of kingly hair. Noni said,

—The watch goes underwater?

—The watch goes everywhere, he said, emerging, as she handed him a towel. His penis, that she hadn't seen in ages, looked smaller than she remembered, fatherly almost. She blinked away a tear, missing all the men she'd lost. The *idea* of men, really.

Then he took the watch off, and placed it around her wrist. And her entire body coursed with the touch of his hand, and the bright metal of his most prized possession.

—It fits, he said. It becomes you.

—It's beautiful.

—It is, it is, he said, and she felt she was losing him to the only god he knew, the god of men who had come before him.

But then he looked her in the eyes. It was one of those moments; Noni could have charted her whole life by the fire of moments like those. He loved her, he loved her not, he loved her.

—Harry, she said, cutting off the moment. It was too much and she had learned over the years, it was better to cut it off before he did. She couldn't survive otherwise.

—Yes, my dear?

—It came to me, maybe overnight, but it dawned on me in the shower. I have an end game.

—Oh, your film?

—The end game is to turn it blue. You see? This county.

—The county, he repeated. These ghosts, he said.

She nodded and then he blinked, and he nodded. It was amazing to behold. When Harry approved, it made one feel like a champion.

Since then she'd been working hard on the project. It had been coming along beautifully. None of the townspeople would know what hit them, and of course she would have to move when the movie came out, but for now it was the work part, the easy part for her, the anonymity and the grace. Now, of course, she had even more space, she had all the time in the world to make it great. She'd always had time, though.

Her friend Susanna was mother to a precocious four-year-old. Su was always scraping for minutes, patching them together into some semblance of a career. She is very fast, and very fearless, Su said of her daughter. Her skill outpaces her brain, so I have always to watch her. I have to watch her and let her be at the same time. My mother-in-law hates the parts of her that are me. You don't need to say *cheese* every time you take a picture, like your mother. I heard her say this.

Noni would smile. Everyone in the world had children. Even though Noni had no experience of her own, she intimately understood what Susanna meant about scraping the minutes. She was a keen observer of others' routines. She absorbed their stories. Harry had said that was the kind of thing that would make her a workhorse in the field but never a genius.

Susanna was forty. Now that she was fifty-six, Noni found herself drawn to women younger than herself. Her age group was withered, allowing their intelligence to slough off, and make way for comfort. When Noni had been in her early twenties, she'd also hung around forty-year-olds. Such as Harry, who was forty, when she met him. Noni herself was perennially forty, much like Harry had been perennially sixty. He'd been sixty when he was forty and he was sixty at the end, at seventy-four, in his casket. Glowering, impressive. She'd wanted him still, his cool body. She'd touched her finger to his big wrist; she dared touch nothing else, for Marian was lurking, as the widows of womanizers must.

But now there was this envelope in her possession, with the whispery little slip inside, that was like a lottery ticket. It would be the end of Marian, Noni guessed. It would be the end of whatever fairy tale women like her had been allowed to dream. Their whole crystal lives. Their navy jackets, their frequent travels with big leather boxes. Noni spoke French, her native Lithuanian, some Italian; she'd had residencies in Sydney, Croatia. She'd shot a film in the bowels of Paraguay. She'd lived in a tent for a month in the Arctic. She was worldly and because of her skills in absorption she could talk for hours with almost anyone from any walk of life, from any corner of the world. But women like Marian woke up gleaming. They had messages waiting for them at hotels in Venice.

It had taken Noni many years to stop wishing she'd been a woman like that. The same kind of woman as his first wife. The kind of woman Harry would have seen fit to marry. As it happened, Noni was neither the type he married nor the type he recklessly fucked, like the reporter from the *Guardian*, or any number of barmaids, students, mordant fellow alcoholics at his meetings. No, Noni was different. Neither gleaming nor wrecked. She was broken but perennially glued together. A case study of a survivalist. Poor, immigrant parents, a chain-link childhood in Newark, New Jersey. Her father, a self-loathing giant who worked eighteen hours a day unloading container ships and butchering pigs. Her mother, too prim for her station, enraged by the life that had swallowed her whole, who'd withheld affection in such a blockbuster way that it took Noni far too long to call it abuse; that, even now, all these years later, with all the accompanying psychoanalysis, she could still recall how her mother would say, My little lady, now and again when Noni emerged freshly showered before bed. There's my little lady, in her special bathrobe. Come here, Mommy's little lady. How, she wondered, could that epithet coexist with a woman who had been, by all other accounts, unable to love?

And now as she spliced some footage, of Luke the brawny crane operator and Elda the horse-queen of Woodville, Noni kept glancing out of the corner of her eye to the envelope on the butcher block. It looked bursting, like a tornado in a frame, like something she both deserved and could not imagine meriting. All her blank life she'd waited on a gift like this one, but now that she had it, she felt it was too much. It wasn't right. After years of eating at bars alone, wishing after something she wanted more than her own continued health, now she felt flagrant, hot faced. Irrationally blessed.

———————

When Noni was sixteen, she'd entered the Guinness Win Your Own Pub in Ireland contest a fantastic number of times. Each entry was fifty words or less about why Guinness was the perfect pint. She had always been good with language, impressive even. There were star writers and thinkers at her school, but Noni was never counted among them. Her intelligence was not showy. It was the kind best suited to emails. To contests. If she won, then everyone at school, plus her mother and her father, they would all find out who she was. This quiet girl—who knew nothing about drinking beer, but who could craft so many unique fifty-word essays on the subject that she'd win her very own bar in the spilling countryside of County Kerry—was bigger than their approximations. She didn't want to be superlative so much as she wanted her world to feel small, myopic.

She didn't win the contest, and what happened was almost worse than losing, the way it seemed to inform much of her future. One of her entries placed in the top twenty-five, when only the top ten advanced, had their names printed up in the local papers, et cetera. She received a form letter letting her know she'd impressed the judges and should try again next year. The same thing happened with every fellowship she went up for, every award, every visiting scholarship. She always impressed the judges, but it was always a very competitive field. Much the same thing could be true of the men she'd dated. She had three times been the woman a man dated before the woman he actually married. It was as though she were a marriage fluffer, priming them for the big show.

Susanna, who thought she knew Noni very well, said that the reason none of the men stuck was because Noni had never come unstuck from Harry. With Su, at her kitchen table in Harlem with her daughter's face smudged with avocado and her little fingers greased with cheap cheese, Noni balked, got pissed or silent or laughed it off, depending on whether or not they were drinking wine. But privately, Noni had to agree. She might take it even further, in her most transparent hours, and admit that the reason she was not a famous documentarian was because of Harry, too. Noni gave up being an ingenue to be something like dryer lint. She remembered nearly every day, the heady, misty mornings in Paris. Instead of focusing on her work, instead of giving all of herself to her vision, she lived in the shadows of the past. A year, was it? A year of being his quiet piece. A year of venison and wine and his naked heft, the hips of an elephant he said himself. There had ever been the feeling of coming from a cold place into a warm one, from the stone cold of Paris in winter to his fire-baked room, from a bracing shower in his naked bathroom to a funnel cake of sweating flesh in his king-sized bed.

By the time they'd both made it back to Manhattan, Harry'd got married to Helene and made four more films, each more celebrated than the last. His best work from that humming period, titled *Buskers*, not so much about buskers themselves but the economics of specific blocks in Paris, Cleveland, and Dubai, had been so lauded that even Noni, for all her admiration of him, became frustrated with the business, with the way of men, who could have multiple children by several wives and still churn out copious product, never having to answer along the way for the time they spent away from their progeny, or divulge the reason they never had them at all.

It was during that time, the fifteen years when Harry was married to Helene, that Noni dated the three near grooms. And the reason, one might posit, that none of those suitors stuck, was not so much because Noni was pining after Harry, not because she was so much in pain; the more accurate fact was that those years were largely analgesic. Noni knew from the start that Helene was not going to last, and so she meandered about, staying just close enough. If she was destined to be a runner-up, to have to try again next year, then so she would wait until Harry's thin marriage to his Bergdorf blonde wasted away to nothing, as almost everyone expected it to. And along the way Helene tried to shut Noni out, and Harry saw less of her when it was required, but mostly they kept up their ways, their banter, their scones, their walks through the park, their occasional spicy glasses of wine in the subterranean Japanese bar near his studio.

So truth be told, Noni hadn't lost Harry to Helene. And it wasn't any of the tarts during his first marriage, or the little breakaways that came after. Noni knew very well, she'd lost Harry to Marian.

—This new woman I've been seeing, her name is Marian, she likes rear entry, Harry told Noni at the swollen wood bar top of their Japanese cellar.

—Are you serious?

—Oh, yes. She is a very classic WASP. Like Helene without the banality. Pearls and pink silk slips. But she loves the back door. She opens up to it. Like a flower.

Noni had been forty-four then. And Harry, sixty-four. His hair completely gray, patrician. At the height of his relevance. In his fly fisherman's vest and his roomy pants. His watch, glinting in the star-light of his eyes. His great beard stunk of gravy, leftover juices, as he sipped his plum wine mere inches from her lips. She'd been biding her time, waiting out the slew of whores who had followed the divorce, waiting for him to grow tired, as she knew he would, of the young students with their black eyes and dumb theories, of the barmaids and their ignorant lust, of the worshipful and the indifferent, of all the wrong women who were not Noni, who did not understand him, who were not his equals, who couldn't look over his work and make deft suggestions for improvement while coherently praising his in-imitable style.

But now this. Something about his tone, the way he dropped his voice, the way he stroked his beard. Noni knew. She felt her heart tear itself away from its moorings. It made her feel young, in truth—as young as she had never been—that it was the first time she'd felt the woe of love. She felt stupid and impaled. And the stake came through the other end, out her back, a mere week later, when Harry insisted Noni come out to meet Marian. She dressed in a white tee and a pair of expensive blue jeans she'd purchased for the occasion. All her life she'd been dressed too formally to meet other women. And Noni had historically felt overreaching. This time, she thought, this time, *I* will be the *deshabille*.

She entered the bar, a long corridor of mirrors and lights, and from far off saw Harry in a suit, and his new woman in an off-the-shoulder black gown, scalloped emerald heels. As she drew closer, Noni saw that her red hair was vivid, natural. Plush lips. Sensual eyes, so slinky as to appear deceitful. A WASP, yes, but not run-of-the-mill. Thirty-six, a tiger age, ripened and wise. Marian was a match for him; Noni knew it right away. The whole evening he kept his giant hand on her hip. They participated in the sort of conversational fucking that Noni had only experienced the very first night with Harry, at an outdoor café in Montmartre where some fellow students could not help but feel uncomfortable by the sooty liaison that was budding before their eyes.

Within a year they were married at City Hall; a reception followed in the bready basement of Harry's favorite restaurant in the West Village, a private dining table by the ovens that fit their thirty closest friends. Noni was invited, of course, but she made an excuse about a teaching engagement and took the weekend to visit Paris. She'd somewhat planned on killing herself, and then the usual happened. One wakes up, and it isn't so bad, and the illusion follows that the progression of days will rise up from bankrupt to decent. Anyway, the truth is the night one makes a suicide pact with oneself is not as bad as the days that precede it, and the ones that follow. When the pact is metabolized by the surviving hours.

And so Noni returned to New York to wait out this union, too. But this time she was too *déprimé* to date. She could only find the words in French to describe her conditions. *L'appel du vide.*

She remained as close to Harry as ever. Perhaps closer yet. She began a strict Pilates regimen, five days a week. On the weekends she walked the streets of lower Manhattan, seeking out inspiration for the next project, as well as rangy thighs. Noni did not have a body like Marian's, or like any of the tall horses Harry went for—she was compact, like a jockey—but she could become the best version of herself. She would lengthen and tone and achieve until he was ready for her again. Helen Gurley Brown had said that she didn't mind waiting a long while before meeting the man of her dreams. She was, in fact, becoming the woman of *his* dreams in the meanwhile. For this tumultuous, desperate period, Noni lived under the debrided warmth of aspirational quotes like these.

One of her other strategies was to get close to Marian, herself. But whereas Helene was troubled by Noni's existence, Marian appeared largely indifferent. She cocked her neck in such a way, like Noni was something she could barely see down there. And nothing Noni could do could charm her. Sometimes Noni spoke highly of herself and Marian would cock her neck and glitter her eyes and Noni would feel like a boorish failure, or they would both arrive at an event in the same general outfit—a tunic dress for one Southampton affair—and Noni would feel like an old slob. She would, in fact, think: What would Marian wear to this event? And then she would try to dress in something more evolved.

Yes, Marian was formidable. Raised in a five-bedroom Greek colonial in Savannah, Georgia, the daughter of a man who would have at one time been a plantation owner. They had much Black domestic help, who would have at one time been slaves. Noni suggested to Harry a documentary about his wife's family, titled *Modern Planters*. Harry shook his head, laughed.

The truth was, Noni was terrified of Marian. Not only of her hold over Harry, but of her hold over Noni herself. Marian was not brilliant by any means, but she was able. Perfect in almost every way. Glowing skin, no errant black hairs on the chin. It boggled Noni's mind that women like these not only grew up rich, but their faces and bodies appeared to know they were being born into noblesse. Women like Marian made Noni believe in caste systems. In her own decrepitude. But, just like the little girl who entered the contest, it didn't make Noni any less motivated.

The ignorant aspects of Marian, even those could fell Noni. Women like Marian recycled old narratives; if, for example, you said you had once taken the wrong route to the home in Roxbury, even if you were only lying, having been late to a dinner because you were obsessing over your makeup, you would forever after be Noni, who did not know direction.

At the party in Southampton, Marian had been standing around with her friends, other women who skied Chamonix and played golf in Évian. Speaking of one of their acquaintances, Marian said, She has skin like a February pumpkin.

Noni had stood there, on a lawn so neat. Her stomach rumbled with the green wine sloshing in her empty belly, and she shivered to imagine what they might say about her.

Eventually, Marian and Harry's union did lose its veneer, as all unions do. It took a good five years, but he returned to fucking around. Yet this time he retained his allegiance to the woman at home. Propriety. He fucked one-offs and foreigners. The occasional runway model. But he always came home to Marian. Perhaps, he told Noni, winking, it's the back door that I come home to.

He continued to hold Noni's ovaries in his fist. Gradually his eyes returned to her, as well, to the way he waited for her to love his new works. And she felt OK again, enough to keep breathing. But every minute of her life was filled with a thought of Marian, in the background, with her long toes. Tall, and Pentecostal.

But now, but now. Noni had this slip of paper.

===

In her kitchen the morning of the reading, Noni fried herself a blue farm egg and mopped up the warm yolk with a slice of whole-grain bread. The kitchen was a small square with a linoleum floor and white cabinets with pine trim, sad and inefficient, a kitchen where disaster was bound to happen.

She showered and shaved. Trimmed her graying pubic hair. Harry liked bushes and nearly every man Noni had been with since had wanted the opposite. Wimpled, bare, tiny. She wondered what Marian was like down there. Roaring or demure, perhaps a fleur-de-lis braided with curling vines of thyme.

When Noni walked outside to her car she saw a truck there, laying hay down where the rains had scalped the grass from the perimeter of the drive. This was one of the troubles of renting homes from those who owned them. Maintenance workers came at any time they wanted; you were never given notice. The workers themselves had no respect for you, you were not the one paying them, and yet they saw you as an extension of their employer, a douchebag all the same with your car that was yet nicer than theirs. An impostor, you were, to the throne.

—Good morning, Noni called out to the man who seemed in charge. A bull-faced man with the same heft of Harry, but without the wealth to his clothing and demeanor.

—I'll move my truck, he said.

It's not your truck, Noni thought. He was angry at her presence, her need to get out of the driveway and teach her class or whatever useless thing he imagined her doing; it meant he was garbage. It made Noni feel like she should be late to her appointments. Like she was in the wrong. At the same time, she thought, Why didn't you just move *your* truck sooner? Why not park it out of the way, just in case the resident needs to leave?

As she drove over the apron, she smiled and waved and he did not wave back.

The day was bright, stony. Harry had died, a month ago to the day, on a morning that foretold of more mornings like these. That day had begun much this way for Noni, leaving her house to teach a class, driving past the blue-collar workers who cut hedges with limp Winstons hanging from their dark lips. She'd known, from miles away, that it was over. He'd been sick for six months, the liver of course, his condition worsening, it seemed, by the day. But she did not actually hear until that night, from social media, from friends of Marian's, and then the following morning, the obituary in the *Times* and the *Post* and the more familial ones on the documentary websites, and none of them, not one, mentioned Noni.

She drove the country roads that would lead her onto the Merritt and then into the city. A beautiful drive on any morning, but certainly in the fall, when the leaves ferment. She passed the Bethlehem Fairgrounds and remembered with stinging clarity the day Harry had taken her to the State Fair. Roasted nuts. Lambs. Jesus Christ, the best. They arrived early in the day and stayed through the evening. At night it turned chilly, so he bought her a Baja from a Mexican woman with plaited eyebrows. They watched a Civil War reenactment, four men gathered around a coal fire, warming their hands and acting desperate. The hope of the State Fair, Harry said to Noni, the fucking American hope! All around them, girls in belly shirts and black Nikes, tractor pulls, the heartbreaking pony pulls, young boys in overalls roping steer, Noni unsure of which was sadder—the boys or the cows—golden blue-ribbon tomatoes, ears of corn so long and imposing, elephant rides, camel rides, ponies led on a swivel by men who had been born to die. Harry and Noni watched all of it with the detached intellectualism that was the birthright of people like themselves. Where had Marian been that day? San Francisco, yes. Kentfield, to be exact. Women like her were always in the right places you hadn't even heard of yet. Just when you thought Paris in the spring was right, there was someplace else to go in March.

They ate Hummel hot dogs and lascivious corn on the cob and apple fritters. Noni's chin was yellow with four different types of oleic acid. Harry's beard was a map of his evening. They did not go back to his house and fuck. Noni felt so good that she was able to play it coy. She felt he loved her that night, that the pendulum had begun to swing. She took the last train home into the city, saying she had to work. But that was the day she decided to move to the country.

There was always a day like that, when you fall in love with a place and you think that this was all along the only thing missing. The place you belonged. The sun will always fall this way. The people will always smile, they will be American Indian and American American, and I won't ever question who they are inside their big boots and behind their smiles.

Now as she passed the fairgrounds, she felt for the first time in the two years since the fair as good, as strong, as powerful, as self-actualized, as she had felt that day. The power over her own life. It was a lie, of course; the power still came from somewhere outside her. It came, now, from this slip of paper, from this meeting to which she was driving.

Noni would walk into the lawyer's office, staid and smelling of nothing that needed. Marian would walk in after, like her kind did. She would be dressed in cream wool and riding boots. The two women, having never been rivals in any real sense, would suddenly be something more deeply polar than either could have imagined. Gladiators, in the postprandial, postapocalyptic catacombs of Manhattan—a Manhattan that had suffered the death of one of its glitterati. Manhattan, of course, would return to itself, but not for another widowing month. And Noni would look at Marian and Marian would look at Noni and they would be seated and the lawyer would state the thing they both already knew:

Harry had left Noni his watch. The Rolex, with its blue hands and its counting down of the world. Four hundred thousand dollars, but the money was immaterial. It was his prized possession. It had been his father's, and his father's father's before him. He wore it during lovemaking, during infrequent showers and naked night swims. He stopped just short of claiming it had magical powers.

And today, in his Madison Avenue lawyer's office, Marian would have to look at Noni, and Noni would feel a tremendous guilt, that this man they had both loved, whom Noni had loved exponentially more, had loved the right woman back. All along, and finally, and forevermore. After decades of being second, third, fourth runner-up, Noni was at last number one. The blue-ribbon girl. All of the polite, subtle rejections of her life would evaporate. This was her pub in Ireland; it was her sunshine-colored tomato. Her mother, for whom she was never truly a little lady, would have to recognize, down in the gray of her grave—Noni was somebody's now, at last. It was too late in only the simplest way, the most corporeal way. In fact, the greatest freedom had come from this gift. Noni, now, did not love Harry as much as she had in life. She'd been liberated from her obsession by his final gift. This was the freedom women like Marian had known their whole lives and now Noni would know it, too. And Marian would know what it was like to be indentured to your own limitations. The ancillary gift, perhaps the best of all, was the most bittersweet: Noni was freed to feel pity for Marian. Sympathy for the woman who stood six inches above her. Her stomach churned with it.

===

Marian, who lived mere blocks from the offices of Spar, Worth, and Lenstein, wouldn't need to leave for the reading for another two hours, and so she sat in her chair, that had once been Harry's chair, that she had hated, like she hated nearly all of the garish pieces he purchased. The Louis XIV settee, for example. The end-of-days end tables.

Not the actual last day, but a few days before it, the famous documentarian sat in the very same chair—lying in it, nearly—and said to his stately wife, But what does it do to you, Marian, really?

Marian sat opposite him, in a canvas dress she wore because it made her feel like she was in the afterworld already. She smoked, because she had begun smoking since the diagnosis; it truly felt, ironically, the only healthy thing to do. She took a long Marian drag and said, Nothing, Harry; I suppose, that it does nothing.

—In French, Harry began, we have a word for—

—We, darling?

—The French have a saying, for letting a woman win a cold dish.

—Yes, I am familiar.

—Marian? Harry said, in his lover's voice, and he sent his eyes to her. In this state, finally, she could see him as the man that he was. It had taken a complete decimation of his body for her to not see all the women in his eyes, all the whores, who buzzed like flies around his dung. All the childish praise he'd sought his whole life, from tiny people, hangers-on. Finally, she saw only Harry, the man she had always known, the man she knew he would always be. She was raised by women who understood how to live with the X-ray of the man. It was the only feminist thing to do, if you were not a lesbian.

—Yes, Harry, she said, and her voice was bored, her manner detachedly conciliatory. The cigarette was blissful; the day was magnificent. She had not cried yet, not in the past six months, but she could tell today was the day it would come.

—Let the poor creature think it, Marian. She needs it, don't you see? It is just one thing.

And Marian looked at his wrist, at the metal that was a part of him. And she looked at the dog on the floor, blue-gray and handsome. She'd never owned a bad dog in her life; they were all like this creature—healthy, divine, and dutiful. Marian hadn't asked to be born this way, the sort of woman for whom life was comprised more of decisions than of reactions. In the days to come there would be a hundred thousand things. Questions and cards and invitations and unsolicited, extraordinary love. The end of Harry would be the beginning of many other lines and paths, and her grief would be the only lonely thing she would tend to, in peaceful moments, in dressing gowns—a fern in her bedroom, rising from the blond loam to greet the penitent sun.

AMERICAN GIRL

THE POLITICIAN WAS BEAUTIFUL AND THE TALK SHOW HOST WAS heavy. This was the first thing everyone noticed about them, both adjectives rendered more acute when they stood beside each other.

—I can't believe he blanks her, said an aide in the politician's office. Like everyone else, the aide was in love with him. He had the kind of nervous brown eyes that all women adored. He was charming but reasonably downtrodden. His parents were poor, he himself was mostly poor, but he had friends in high places. Underneath the aw shuckserie, he was as brightly ambitious as all young, good-looking men are.

—I feel like he closes his eyes the whole time, said another young woman. Both were brunettes whose mothers had taught them not to put out too early. They were looking at a blurry image of the politician and the talk show host on the television screen above. They'd been snapped by TMZ eating dinner together, on the same side of the table, at a restaurant on the water.

—Nobu, said the aide, sneering. I can't believe he went there.

—Her call, for sure, said the other. Anyway, she's picking up the tab.

Both girls laughed.

Margherita refilled the hot sauce bottles at every table. She used a bar mop to polish away the smudges. She refilled the wire bowls on the suspended shelves with Meyer lemons and avocadoes. The hot sauce was made in-house using florid cayenne peppers from the garden outside. She used to give a fuck about tiny beauties like that.

The first customer of the day was Jeff, who worked for a beachy hedge fund in Marina del Rey and lived in one of the zealous condos there. He came all the way out to Venice, he said, for the smoked fish and egg sandwich. But Margherita knew it was for her. Even so, he had never tipped more than fifteen percent.

—Hey, star, he said as he sat down in her section. She had the window section, the best section.

—Early start at the office? Margherita said, rubbing his bottle of hot sauce.

—Very funny, Jeff said. It was noon on a Monday. He wasn't fat, but his face had too much skin.

—The usual?

—Could you call it something less bitchy?

—The early day at the office?

He smiled. She jabbed her chin at him. She'd let him take her out for early drinks once. Before the sun had even set, he'd got drunk and raspy, paying some hipster twenty bucks for a menthol cigarette. He'd leaned into her neck and said, I want to fly you to Rome tomorrow, seriously.

Back behind the counter, Hiro the imaginary chef had already assembled the sandwich, using the gravlax that looked like the foreskin Margherita once encountered at a bris.

She dawdled, checking her phone. An email had come through from Phillip's campaign. They were always in Courier New. The paragraphs were single sentences and the sentences were brief. He wrote everything himself, even though now he had a speechwriter. He was a poor speller, but nobody cared about that. Each of his fundraisers had a signature drink. He knew that merely adding mint to something staid lent a sense of valor.

You are cordially invited to a fundraiser with Phillip Coover on May Day from 4 p.m. to 10

At the Home of Marie Land

Music . . . Walrus, African drums

Food . . . spit-roasted birds and mizuna with watermelon radish

Drink . . . margaritahs with orange peel and mint

One hundred dollars ahead, two at the door

love to see you

The *h* was for her, she knew, and the *love to see you* was for her and like seventeen others. Margherita unsubscribed from the mailing list. She was asked her reason for unsubscribing. *Too many emails?* No, the campaign sent the perfect amount. *No longer relevant?* In fact, she worried they would always be relevant. She selected Other and clicked Submit.

A message flashed: *The comment section cannot be left blank.*

OK, she wrote in the comment box, and sent it through again. Then she brought the smoked-fish sandwich to Jeff, remembering how, at the bris, the infant's family served capers and bagels and chickpeas alongside a platter of layered and glistening lox. Margherita didn't eat the lox because she hadn't known at the time that that's what it was.

——————

—I am fucking in love with him, said the famous actress to nobody.

She was old, though, too old. She was forty-one in the press, forty-six in real life. She was old enough that the computer could not discover her lie. That was old.

The famous actress was not terribly famous. Once she had been. Now she just had great cardigans, fantastic leather sandals for shushing across the sand on her eighty-foot stretch of Malibu beachfront.

He'd been over three times, for parties, and on the third time he dropped the hint. No! She did; it was her. She said, If you ever want to use my place. His eyes grew so big she wanted to hit them. She wanted to pee in his eyes.

He wanted a son. All men did. Maybe he wanted a daughter. She could still do it, give one to him, but for how much longer. She was stork thin; that was all she had these days. Thinness and money and coffee for free.

She'd heard the rumors. She'd gifted him her PR girl. That dolt from Indiana, Mandy Sue, told the famous actress about the talk show host a month ago, before anyone knew. Mandy Sue knew everything. What bars did the idiot go to? What shitty place in West Hollywood, where all the underlings went and shared the gossip of the people for whom they bought Cerignola olives?

Her dress was laid out for the event. Rose-gold chiffon. It was laid out on the bed like a chalk outline. The talk show host suddenly had more money than she did and was younger. Not young, but younger.

She was not pretty. Her weight notwithstanding, the talk show host could never pass. But she was relevant in a way the famous actress could never be anymore. The actress had always been too fine boned to be relevant.

The actress thought that if people got the people they wanted just by sheer force of wanting them, then she would get her man. The only man, after all, she had ever loved. She had waited to try for another child until she found the right one. Why had he come so late, and why was he leaving so early? Why? she said to the glass walls of her balcony, above which she could taste the salt of the ocean and the weightlessness of God.

———

It had been a month since the talk show host discovered her magical power. *Re*discovered, in any case. She remembered the precise moment in Gjusta, where the gorgeous Croatian worked.

Cremora—named for the nondairy creamer her mother loved— had just ordered the smoked-fish sandwich, with the bread on the side. This was useless; she always ate the bread, anyway, after she'd cleared the plate of capers and slick fish.

The waitress, Margherita—the most incandescent, bustiest brunette one could imagine—approached, carrying Cremora's deconstructed fish sandwich. In that moment, Cremora felt all her pounds and self-debasement. She took a sip of her sparkling limeade and cursed God and her father and an entire society that prized women like this waitress over Cremora. Even though this waitress likely lived in Silver Lake, drove a shit car, and roomed with busboys, she was gorgeous. More exotic, shorter, and sloppier than a model. Gorgeous, medium rare.

But that wasn't the worst of it.

Every five years or so in Los Angeles and New York there was one man everyone wanted. For the past two years it had been Phillip Coover, State Representative from California's Ninth District.

Cremora had first seen him at a dying director's birthday party in San Miguel de Allende, six months prior. He was good-looking but not absurdly hot. She walked into the director's kitchen while Phillip was replacing the giant water jug in the dispenser. He hadn't known anyone would see him. Cremora was struck by that humanity. Kind men were in fashion again, after many centuries.

He'd been known to those who mattered for several years. Cremora herself had just reached her relevancy prime, but she'd been too busy nursing the wound a famous actor had opened in her.

—Hi, Phillip had said, startled. I've been wanting to meet you. I'm a huge fan.

That afternoon Cremora had been wearing a Loup Charmant beige-striped caftan over a Jade one-piece. The whole outfit, including the toquilla-straw hat on her head, cost twenty-three hundred dollars. It was the bare minimum amount she had to spend on an outfit in order to leave the house. On her podcasts she extolled the virtues of womanhood, of feeling proud at any size. Across the country lady bus drivers and teachers with endometriosis counted her as their savior, the reason they were able to climb out from the trenches of annulment and binge eating.

—I'm sorry, I don't know your name.

—Phillip Coover, I'm your representative.

His eyes fucked her. They did not merely get on top but rather picked up her whole body and lowered her down on top of them. Just like that, the pain of the famous actor was gone, replaced with the herpetic fever of a new crush. In the past several years Cremora had become extraordinarily wealthy, and well loved by the sorts of women she never wanted to hang out with. But the way she developed crushes was the same as it had always been. Furious, childlike.

For the rest of that weekend she watched him swim in the small saltwater pool and eat scallop ceviche and be gallant. Thereafter, she spent months triangulating his whereabouts, bumping into him at events. She also worked on getting more famous, and more interested in politics. She'd been hoping that sheer obsession and maneuvering might get her a date with him. But she had not counted on magic.

Cremora went to Gjusta that fateful day because she knew he would be there. She paid her assistant to be a creep. But when she got there, she saw him with Margherita. It was clear they had fucked. Not only that, it was clear they didn't use condoms and had spent at least one weird Palm Springs weekend together.

Something in Cremora snapped. Some rage at the idea of exquisiteness. It had started, of course, many moons ago, with the first woman her father brought home after Cremora's mother died the sad, brittle, bony, blond death of the diseased young mother.

One morning, mere months after the funeral, ten-year-old Cremora woke up and a strange lady was making eggs on their dirty white stove. Her father was making coffee and humming. The woman was gorgeous; it was the first thing Cremora thought. She felt like she'd betrayed her mother with the thought.

—This is my friend, Patricia, her father said, beaming.

The woman wore a shapeless linen dress and her long black hair was witchy and stunning.

For weeks Cremora thought about suicide. Then she recalibrated. When she'd been even younger, and her mother had first got sick—

though at first everyone just thought she was tired because she was always sleeping late—Cremora taught herself how to wake up for school on her own. All she had to do was think of the precise time, 6:30 a.m., see the numbers in her head, and hone in on them. She wrote the digits on a slip of paper over and over, until her whole brain was taken up with the time. Like magic every morning her eyes would slip open at 6:30.

She appropriated this technique for Patricia. In the library after school she would go and research rare diseases. After several weeks she settled on Hemorrhagic Proctocolitis. She would stare at images of it in the encyclopedia and in medical journals. She would draw pictures of a beautiful black-haired woman bleeding out of her anus. She would watch Patricia at the house, sitting on the white couch Cremora's mother died on, and imagine a giant pool of blood materializing under her bottom. She even made a vision board and put the letters of Patricia's name all across the canvas alongside case studies of the disease and bright splotches of red Sharpie. She hid it under her bed and dreamed nightly about rectal bleeding.

Within six months, Patricia was diagnosed with bladder cancer. Which, Cremora figured, was close enough. Her father left, because he couldn't do it again, he said, lose another woman. Nothing much changed as far as Cremora was concerned; her dad never took her bowling, or even out to dinner just the two of them. Eventually he got a new girlfriend, a redhead with buck teeth who stuck around. Cremora didn't have it in herself to hate the new lady. She was saddened by this. The evanescence of obsession was like a sagging tit.

What followed, instead, was years of hating herself. Of wanting things from men that she couldn't articulate. Of eating too many all-natural snacks, like vegan cheddar doodles and onion chips from the islands.

In Gjusta that day she wasn't even actively trying to do anything. She was just so livid about another beautiful woman serving eggs. She could feel it surging through her body, the decades of never once liking a man who liked her back. Something inside became very clear. She didn't need to concentrate for weeks like last time, because all the debasement was wound up like a lawn mower.

Exactly then was when Phillip Coover looked at her. It was like the waitress evaporated.

—Hello! he said, waving from across the room. He came over to Cremora's table, giant coffee cup in hand, and sat down. Cremora watched the waitress's eyes go holy shit and then she watched them water. Go to Morocco, Cremora shouted in her head, laughing. Go to Chefchaouen and walk the streets with your swimmy black hair!

Anyhow, that was the moment the magic worked. The politician was smitten. He was hers. They were inseparable ever after.

―――――

—Please? Summer said.

—No, Margherita said. You go.

—I can't go without you. There will be hot guys there.

—You care more about hot guys than my pain.

—Dude, get real. Every single chick cares more about hot guys than another woman's pain. Fuck. I care more about whether or not I ordered the Dior Show in waterproof or not. I hate returning shit.

They were in the café. Two waitresses. Summer had throwback highlights. Margherita was more serious, because she was from another country originally. The fundraiser was that night, at the formerly famous actress's house in Malibu.

Summer was doing all of Margherita's side work. Margherita

knew that if she let Summer Saran Wrap the fish tins that would be the end. She would have to go. She began to cry.

—Fuck, man, for serious? Summer exasperatedly looked away from her reflection in the steel prep table, pretending to be shocked that Margherita was crying.

—Fuck off.

—You fuck off, said Summer. You can have literally anyone.

But Margherita knew that wasn't true. She was beautiful and smart and would someday be a wonderful mother, but she knew that wasn't enough. Loving herself wasn't even enough. These days, women had to be a million things. Being beautiful was passé. A successful man was better perceived if he had an ugly wife. It meant he was full of character. How many times had she fucked Phillip? They had never fucked. They had always made love. He was the type, soft and negligent, to make love by default. With his tongue that tasted of celery, marvelous nothing.

Then came the day in the café—it wasn't a café; it was a deli and a smoked-fish market and a butcher shop and a workspace and a juice bar; cafés these days were like women; they had to be a million perfect things, shiny and cozy and utilitarian at once—when the talk show host walked in and Margherita lost Phillip to her. It was like a spell had been cast. It was the day 1955 was replaced by the machinelike, shapeless future.

From that day forward he still texted her simpering little nothings, pictures of piglets and goats and cracked knuckles of crab, but she hadn't seen him since. She knew it was fine, she hadn't been a girlfriend. She'd been both more and less. She knew it was trite to want to be a girlfriend. She'd been his lover. And one day, when it was safe, he would slink back, because of her ass and her lips. Beauty never went out of style in the vacuum of the penis. And she would let him make love to her, because there were so few good men.

—Anyway, it's not about men, you know, Summer was saying. I want a baby. I want a fluffy little girl who I can raise to be a curly-headed lesbian. I want to raise a daughter with blades on her tongue who will give blow jobs to all the guys that hurt me. Us, she added, putting an arm around Margherita, who had begun wildly weeping. All the guys who hurt *us*.

—If only we could band together, Margherita agreed.

But Summer did not hear; she was applying lipstick in the reflection of a silver creamer.

━━━━━

Cremora got ready for the fundraiser at her bungalow in Venice. She hadn't moved to LA until she could properly do LA. She'd waited until she could afford six grand a month. She'd wanted to avoid complexes with wrought-iron gates and shared, cheap swimming pools. They all had names like Pacific Bay Towers and Ocean Towers. She'd bided her time in Ventura, living in a studio, going to the Vons with coupons in the visor of her Prius. She'd worked quietly and capaciously for five years, attended all yoga happy hours, and followed the right people on Instagram. She started the podcasts with the recording devices perched on her stove and the interviewee sitting in a tight corner next to a mousetrap. The first ones were the most suicidal. The mom from Santa Clarita whose kid died on an escalator. The four-hundred-pound high schooler who said she couldn't figure out how many pills it would take for someone her size and that was always what stopped her.

In the bright lemony light of that filthy kitchen, Cremora knew she'd struck gold. The name, American Girl, had come to her organically. Staring at those women, listening to them, ones showing more rot than she herself had even known, she knew she'd landed smack on the pulse of the nation. The women were dying. They were dying on the inside and Cremora would show that by giving voice to the ones who wanted to kill themselves on the outside.

It was the opposite gender that had always eluded her. It seemed they always wanted something she hadn't thought about. It was like going to the market for tea cake ingredients and coming home without the fucking English breakfast.

But then the magic happened. In the past month she and Phillip had gone to a Lakers game, to Hog Island for oysters and Camembert, and to Joshua Tree, where they fucked under a cactus shaped like a cross. Yes, she had paid for nearly everything, but one day he was going to be a senator. Even if it was magic, it was *her* magic he was responding to. It was like, she decided, a pheromone.

And she was happier than anyone had ever been. She felt all her badness dissipate and pee out of her in the shower. He was beautiful. He made the sunniest of eggs. His smile was as safe and overwhelming as the Sunday crossword. There were no problems. He said, I love you with every piece of me. Nothing he said was ever specific or realistic. She wanted him more than he wanted her. But there were no other problems.

———————

—I read somewhere, said the famous actress to her stylist, that girls who have strong bonds with their fathers become overachievers.

—Hmm, said Brandon, taking a big swig of his silver vape. Everything about him smelled like carrots. He was leaning over her glass balcony and staring at the beach. It was enough for people like him to be able to come to houses like hers a few times a week. What about mothers? he said.

—I feel like mothers are both superimportant and unimportant at once, the famous actress said. She hated that she had started saying things like *I feel like*. She was always trying to be a decade younger. She was meant to be a decade younger.

—Mothers have a lot to do with beauty, Brandon said. They can make you feel like shit in the looks department.

—I really never had a woman champion me, the famous actress said. My agent calling me talented twice in two weeks is probably the best I've ever got from a woman.

—Politics is the new celebrity, said Brandon. He always put her in things she felt cheap in. He liked her hair cheap and big. But she couldn't fire him. You couldn't fire a stylist. It was akin to admitting you hated yourself.

—I'm exhausted, said the famous actress, that there is always a new thing.

—Well, thank God that now it's politics, we need it. The marginalized.

—That's the joke; the marginalized will always be marginalized.

—I'm gay, Brandon said thoughtlessly. This is my moment.

—You've been having your moment for years. Where's the moment for older women?

—Women are having a moment.

—*Young* women are having a moment. Young women always have the moment.

He laughed in hearty agreement. It was too easy to make people poorer than herself laugh. She looked out at the water. Now they were both looking out at the water and talking to it, like one of the countless terrible films she'd been in.

—You love this stupid boy? Brandon said, because she had been depressed for a month. I love him, too, he said.

—I want him, mightily. I never want anyone.

—You could be a dyke.

—Too late. The moment for dykes has passed, too.

—What are you going to do, Marie? Kill yourself?

—Tonight, maybe.

—Don't do it tonight. Do it tomorrow. Tonight is going to be *shiny*. Look at the pool!

Marie looked at the pool. There were real lily pads from India and American Girl dolls riding inflatable swans. Soon there would be Korean girls with terrific bangs and Nigerian girls with racing legs serving *ikura* on *shiso* leaves. A taut bartender was looking up at her like he wanted to fuck her, because that's the way every hot man in this town looked at every powerful woman. She looked at Brandon, who did the same thing. Even gay men were men, after all.

—Darling? Are you going to wear the rose-gold or aren't you? I'll match my cravat to the color, if you do.

———

Margherita handed the keys to her Ford Fiesta over to the valet driver. He stared at her and Summer. Together they were flawless, lime scented.

Why had she come out here? This dust place. She missed the trees cracking in the February of cold places. And the sea in the winter.

Summer went ahead of her. A woman in a pale-pink tuxedo was greeting guests with margaritas at the door.

She and Summer had nothing in common. They had fucked the same man, actually. An Irish football player. It was completely random. He'd never even come into the café. But that was how it was. There were so few men who didn't have red beards or stink of goat cheese and there were so many fantastic women.

There had been one night in Palm Springs when she felt absolutely assured. He'd gone down on her in such a way. They'd eaten sunchokes for dinner and nothing else. Sunchokes roasted in olive oil with giant flakes of salt. He was always looking beyond her. But he had a duty to the country. She believed in it and in him.

Once, she'd helped a young chef get his restaurant off the ground. She'd helped clean the fowl and the fish. She hosed the blood off concrete floors. That man was in Uruguay now, with a restaurant on its own private island.

People like her were not named in the credits. They were invited to all the after parties. Their Instagram accounts glowed with lemon trees and freshly killed pigs and hazy images of themselves beside Atlantic Ocean fire pits. Not once in her life had Margherita ever been left out.

Cremora saw the waitress come in and it stopped her heart. She wore a red dress with a 1980s neckline. It probably cost less than seventy dollars.

She wanted to ask her future husband if the campaign invited the waitress or if he did. But she was not attractive enough to ask those questions. She would only be highlighting her own unattractiveness in light of the Croatian's beauty.

The famous actor she'd loved had fucked her seven times in five nights. There had been no relationship, just a week in Marfa shooting a commercial for autism. She'd been the only famous woman there, and all the grips and PAs were boys or lesbians. There had been the usual drunk talks over sangria in a hot place with big skies, but no real soul digging. But she watched him so much on the screen that she felt she knew him. Men, after all, were easy to know after you fucked them. It was what they withheld when they weren't fucking you that made you think there was more.

One time, in between Patricia and the woman he married, Cremora's father confided in her about his taste in women. He said he liked women who looked like they ate candy. Lollipops, jawbreakers. He liked women who were a little wrecked looking, skinny, meth cheeked, and healthy in the unhealthy sense, like they could survive a holocaust because of their white trash genes. He had, in truth, only said the part about candy, but Cremora put the rest together on her own. Their carpet, growing up, smelled of feet and disease. Her father smelled rich but acted poor, aggressive; he never wanted for women. Her mother was not healthy in the unhealthy sense, but the opposite.

———

—I always wanted a little girl like you, the famous actress said.

She washed two Klonopin and two Ativan down with a spicy glass of grenache. She always drank her own wine at parties. It was the one loving thing she did for herself. Everyone else drank from giant Bota boxes behind the bar. Even the dying director.

The famous actress was talking to her flat belly, caressing it, and laughing. She was on her balcony. Down below, the talk show host gazed happily at the American Girl dolls in the pool. She was on the arm of the man they both loved. The famous actress wondered if any woman had ever been happy for any other woman in the history of the world. With the exception, of course, of their daughters.

—Holy shit, said one brunette to the other, after her boss announced his engagement to the poolside of partygoers.

—What the fuck! said the other.

—No two people have ever been so scared to lose one another, whispered the first brunette, sagely.

—But, said the other, a grim longing in her tone, she's so *fat*.

Phillip saw Margherita walk in with one of her hot friends. His eyes, briefly, swam. She would be fine, he knew; she would marry a personal chef and one random Tuesday in the future when they reunited in Big Sur he would tell her the truth, that he'd loved her best. With an IPA in his hand, he would explain to her about men, who needed to accomplish something in outer space in order to exist.

Later, when the silver stars lit up the ocean and the rain began to fall, Phillip would walk inside Marie's house to use the bathroom and afterward he would walk out to the glass balcony and look out at the revelers, the voters. Soon it would all be his, Los Angeles and then New York, which was harder and also easier at once. Plus all the little places in between with the Kohl's-shopping mothers and the fathers who wanted to kill the men who raped their daughters but instead merely lunged at them in courtrooms, after it was too late.

Phillip wouldn't see the famous actress floating facedown in the pool. It would look like art, like a 1950s scene, with the dolls and the lily pads and the chiffon dress riding up to bare her bony rear. Margherita would be the one to find her; she would fish the older woman out of the water, her fine wrists dripping. Brandon the stylist would be the one to tell Phillip; he would take him by the elbow and lead him away from the mess. I have to protect you from this, Brandon would whisper, his cravat loosened from grief.

Phillip knew that Marie Land had feelings for him, but he didn't know much else. He didn't know about the child of hers who had been stillborn. It wouldn't matter even if he did. He hadn't been the one to put it there. And men never understood loving something that didn't breathe air. They didn't understand loving someone who didn't love you back, even if that person said they loved you. Phillip knew one woman, a former *Bachelor* contestant, hung herself by a vacuum cord because her NBA player boyfriend told her he didn't love her. He told his new fiancée he thought that was insane. The suicidal girl had been on the phone with her mother as she wound the cord around her neck. How could she do that to her family? said Phillip, as though he didn't know what Cremora did for a living.

And as for his fiancée, he had never seen the marks on her wrist because there was now a numerical tattoo on one of them and on the other she wore a bangle made by starving girls in Uganda. He didn't know the word *cancer* was a sore spot. For that matter he'd also never seen the bright white bald spot, the size of a nickel, on the top of her head—a souvenir from the decade she'd pulled her strands out, like a mother gorilla, while watching *Melrose Place*. It made sense that he'd never seen it, because she went through hoops to hide it. Hats, hairspray, even Chanel Giallo Napoli nail polish.

But for now Phillip would not see anything but the ocean. He would not be bothered by the rain. He would be sober because he never drank too much, because what he wanted was always in the future. And he would think about that future, as he always did, every second of every day. For starters, he was confident in his engagement. When he'd slipped the glistening ring on her plump finger, his new fiancée's eyes had sparkled like quartzes. He'd promised himself he would never stop fucking her. She would be like a dog, something friendly he could always count on.

Her name, too, was a sign. It was the name of the blond dust his grandfather spooned into his coffee. Phillip spent all his summers with the man, learning to make wine, learning to make eggs, learning to use a walking stick and all the other shit that was sold on Abbot Kinney now for $495. It was his grandfather and not his father Phillip looked up to, even though it was his father he resembled. It was his grandfather whom Phillip aspired to live like. Dust Bowl poor but Kennedy proud. A man who every day farmed twenty-seven acres in the sandy farmland of Monterey County. Now it was overrun with marijuana plants and Mexican men who wore bandanas across their mouths to keep out the grit. But back when, his grandfather had risen every morning with his coffee and Cremora and a buttermilk biscuit and plowed fields and roped steer and killed pigs and packed giant dips the size of a lesser man's balls. His grandfather, for whom he was named. His grandfather, who did not need anything but his own hands to get ahead.

A SUBURBAN WEEKEND

On a scorching Sunday in late August, Fern and Liv lay out in the sun at Liv's parents' country club. At twenty-seven, they were old to be coming in from the city for the weekend, swimming in the pool and eating chicken salad lunches on the patio, signing the bill to Liv's fat father's account.

But last night was weird—broken rubbers, lukewarm digestifs—and to stay in Manhattan after that kind of night, during a heat wave, would have been too much.

They chose two lounge chairs next to the pool. Little girls splashed and squealed and twiggy boys walked underwater, their palms periscoping like shark fins. Even the children with very long hair didn't need swimming caps at the club. Caps were for the town pool, where the members shed and had split ends.

Club employees in cream polos and khaki shorts jotted drink orders and then took forty minutes to retrieve Diet Cokes with sturdy lemon wedges. The girls looked at their feet, and past their feet to the annoying kids in the water. They looked up and felt the sun on their necks. The suburban sky was a Windex blue, whereas in Manhattan the blue was washed-out, blue like you had just slept with some guy in the same small room in which your best friend had slept with some other guy.

Fern and Liv were always trying to decide who was prettier, hotter, who could bypass the line to get into Le Bain, who looked more elegant drinking *cortados* at a café with crossed legs. The answer flickered, depending on whether they were assessing themselves from far away or up close, and what each was wearing, how her hair looked, how much rest she'd got, and, of course, who had recently been hit on hardest by tall guys with MBAs.

The facts. Fern was skinnier than Liv, but Liv was blond and tall and her breasts were enormous and thrillingly spaced. Liv could have been called chubby in certain circumstances, in jeans or leggings for example, or at power yoga. Fern's face could look misshapen, in weird lighting, with no makeup. Liv had a better chance of being called beautiful, especially by Black guys and Danes. Fern was more often sexy, mysterious. Small, Jewish men liked her. Also, men from any of the Latin countries, and Italians from Jersey or Delaware. Cleft-lipped financiers and Bushwick bloggers. Irish guys went for both girls. Bartenders liked neither.

Fern was reading *The Executioner's Song*; she welcomed the way the heavy book felt against the tops of her thighs. She wanted to be ground down. Liv had one of her graphic novels; she was the funny one, the one who stayed at the bar the latest with the people who were either waiting around to hook up or the alcoholics who never thought it was time to go home. Liv was more the latter. She didn't want to hook up as much as she wanted to *be out*. She made others feel lame for going home before two in the morning.

Fern was thinking about her empty childhood house. Though it was less than three miles away, her family hadn't belonged to this club.

They'd summered at the township pool. They would spread their brown-horse towel and the light-yellow irregular Nautica towel on the hot cement; her parents smoked while she swam. First her father, and then her mother, drew cancer from the wheel of how you will die. Fern imagined this wheel was in a shitty part of London, spun by a man with brown teeth and coke fingernails. Her mother was incinerated just a few months ago.

Now the family home was for sale, plus all of its contents: the Capodimonte statuettes of old Italian men playing bocce, eating speck, licking their dark fingers; the *Encyclopedia Britannica*; her father's marble penholder; the aluminum bowls belonging to Puppy, who lived for four years before getting hit by an Escalade on South Orange Avenue.

Not for sale: the yellowed stacks of *TV Guides* Fern's mother collected, especially the Fall Previews; and a bowl of handmade Venetian candies called *lacrime d'amore*. Tears of love. They were little pellets about twice the size of a peppercorn, fine pastel shells filled with a drop of *rosolio*, an Italian liqueur made from rose petals. They evaporated in your mouth like racy air. When they'd arrived in the mail, all the way from Marghera, Fern's mother cast her leather neck back and cried with joy. Some cousin recently told Fern you could find them out near Newark now, an Italian importer. But by then Fern's mom had already turned gray. *It's the lack of oxygen*, a hipster resident at Saint Barnabas Medical said with confidence. See how our faces are pink? That's oxygenated blood. Your mother's is quickly dwindling. It's like her blood can't breathe.

As though reading aloud from her graphic novel, Liv hummed.

"Uh, uh, uh, uh, oh, oh, ohmygod, ohmygod, ohmygod, *ohmyfuckinggod*!"

Fern laughed. She kicked Liv's considerable calf with her little foot.

—Your sex noises, Liv continued, not joining in the laughter, are ultra-soft-core. HBO circa 1996.

—Ew. Fuck you.

—They're like. Husband pleasing.

—Dude, your kissing noises are pretty homo. *Ooom-wah, ooom-wah.* It sounded like an annoying washing machine.

—What does that even mean?

—In fucking Sears.

—Can you pass me the Pirate's Booty?

Fern tossed Liv the bag of butter-colored food product that Liv's mom kept in their pantry of bright, fat-people items. Fern, who had no parents, loved the pantry. She loved Liv's mom.

—Liv, Liv, Fern said with a Latin accent. You are so glamorous, Liv, when you eat the Booty.

Fern knew that whenever Liv was upset it was best to poke fun harmlessly and, in doing so, incidentally worship her.

Now Liv laughed. How about those Argentineans? she said.

—Jesus Christ, said Fern. My thighs are still quivering.

=====

Last night had begun at the Arthur Ashe Stadium. Round one of the Men's US Open. Liv's father worked in marketing for Mercedes, a platinum sponsor, and had got the girls two good seats to one of the matches. A Swede who was hot versus a Brit who was not. It was luminous and Waspy in the stadium. Ruddy women in hats and men in crisp Bonobos. Cologne, lemon dresses, the occasional Chinatown fan. Some Staten Island dads with clapping hats. The place was mostly packed, but for two empty seats beside the girls. They drank light beers from plastic cups and raised their tanned arms in the air whenever the Swede got a point.

"Fifteen Love," they would preempt the announcer.

Fern wore a red skater dress with a pair of navy espadrille wedges. Liv wore a floral romper and leather flats and made fun of Fern for wearing heels.

—They're not heels; they're wedges.

—Whatever, hooker.

—You're just jealous because I'm not an Amazon and I can wear heels without freaking people out.

"Hey, Fur, why don't you go hook yourself in the boxes? Lots of Deutsche douches looking for a GFE."

—Yum, prime rib under carving lights. Fuck. Should we crash a box?

—I don't know. I keep looking at these two empty seats, imagining the loves of our lives coming in and sitting down.

Fern rolled her eyes; she used to feel the same, but now she was a person who didn't care who sat down beside her. The courthouse, the subway. Maybe if she took the Effexor that she'd been prescribed, she would give a flying fuck.

Two men were suddenly standing above them. The girls looked up, shielding their eyes from the sun. The men were dads, golfers, bald, buzzed.

—These seats taken? said the one wearing a Masters polo from the previous year.

—I don't understand, Fern said. Are they yours?

—No, said the other, holding curly fries.

—Then yes, Fern said, they're taken by the people who paid for them.

But she did the full-body version of batting her eyelashes. The only thing that had lately survived in Fern was a desire to make men want to fuck her. All men. Every single man she saw. Hot dog vendors. UPS drivers across the street. Liv called her a slut. It made Liv angry. A lot of things about Fern made Liv angry. But then, Liv did nice things. She spoke to Fern in Fern's mother's Italian accent, for example.

The guy with the curly fries looked past Fern to Liv.

—Hello, excuse me, are you one of the players? Liv did look like one of the Slavic stars with her white teeth and voracious forearms.

—Yes, she said. But I'm like ninth seed, so.

—Oh, wow! What is it like, at a women's match? Are there a lot less spectators?

—Yeah, about ninety-five percent less.

—That many, wow.

—Yeah. But this year we're giving out Thinx. That's the period underwear. So we're hopeful.

The guy in the polo brought out a newly purchased visor and a black Sharpie and Liv signed the name Paulina Porn-ikova to the lid.

The girls watched some more tennis, yawned, texted, and got up to get another pair of beers, and a jumbo soft pretzel to share.

When they returned, two nice-looking young men were sitting in the spare seats beside them.

—Are you fucking kidding me right now? Liv whispered to Fern.

The boys seemed as pleased as the girls. The dark-haired one was Sebastián and the blond was Axel. They were Argentinean derivatives traders, working in Latin American markets in the city. Sebastián, whose father was an ambassador, wore a Rolex, while Axel was more sporty, with goofy teeth and horny blue eyes. They were both well dressed and vaguely soulless.

They watched the rest of the match together. At some point it seemed both young men wanted Liv, and at another point it seemed they both wanted Fern. Sebastián told them to call him Seb. He was quiet while Axel was hyper. In many ways their relationship to each other mirrored Fern and Liv's. When the match was over they all rode the 7 train back into the city.

—Let's get off here, Sebastián said, as they neared Gramercy. We will have a drink at Pete's Tavern.

They were slightly warmer than American boys, and they paid for all the cocktails without question. Fern knew, for as little or as long as she lived, that she would never fall in love; she thought it was so childish that Liv believed in fairy-tale romance like an idiot. That was why she liked Seb better. He was the colder of the two boys, and he seemed like he could take the girls or leave them, while Axel seemed bent on getting laid.

—It's getting late, Seb said, around eleven. I have a squash game in the morning.

—You are right, Axel said. Let's go up to your place for a nightcap.

—Are you sleeping over?

—Yes, brother, Axel said. Come on, girls, you can see what a bomb site my friend lives in.

Seb's place was right across the street from the bar. The girls were shocked to see it was a studio. Granted, it was a doorman building in a prime location, but the idea of an ambassador's son living in a studio with all his dry cleaning hanging from the rusty rod of his shower dulled the thrill of the hunt.

Seb brought out four mismatched glasses and poured Fernet-Branca.

—OK, he said, it is time for me to collect on my win. Earlier, at the game, they'd bet on the point spread of the game, and the stakes had been that the winner could make a rule, any rule he wanted.

—Do you know what you want? Liv said, rubbing her pink lips around the rim of her glass.

—I think I do, Seb said. He walked into the bedroom section of his studio and came back with a paisley tie. He proposed blindfolding Axel and suggested that both girls should kiss him and Axel would try to figure out which was which and who was better. Seb would go after.

Fern went second, both times. She used a different technique with each boy. With Seb she didn't even touch his body; she just matched her lips to his and kissed lightly and seductively. With Axel, she moved one hand along his waist and brought her other around his neck. Then she sucked on his tongue like a porn star.

Liv kissed both boys the way Liv kissed. Fern knew something about that because she'd once woken in the middle of the night with Liv's mouth on hers. Liv had been holding Fern's hands, like teenagers on a park bench. Liv took a lot of Adderall, which acted like cocaine at high dosages, so she would pass out hard and then do weird shit in her sleep. In the morning Liv, bleary-eyed, said, Yo, man, did you try to make out with me last night? Anyway, Fern knew Liv's kiss style was *true love*.

Axel was more diplomatic, but basically both boys said the second girl was the better kisser.

Liv, of course, was pissed. Fern excelled at most things. It was because Fern wanted to win. It was all she had.

They talked and laughed some more and drank as though the kissing never happened. But the smell of blood was in the air, a slutty rivalry radiating between the girls. Fern assumed it was for Seb, since that was the Argentinean she wanted. When Liv got up to go to the bathroom, Fern turned her face to his and flashed a spiritual *fuck me* gaze.

Eventually it ended up with Fern and Seb in Seb's bed and Liv and Axel on the banana-leaf futon by the door. There was rustling and then there was nothing and then there was the sound of heavy sliding, like repo men in the middle of the night.

—Fur, are you doing it? Liv asked from across the room.

Fern giggled. Seb said, *Shhh*, and they fucked dementedly. She felt more at peace with this boy she barely knew than with Liv, who always needed to know what she was doing, and how she was feeling.

———

The country club pool looked like a giant Blue Hawaiian. That was the cocktail, Fern knew, that caused Liv to fail her bartender exam. It was made with curaçao, rum, pineapple juice, and cream of coconut. Instead of cream of coconut, Liv used sour mix. But that was a Blue Hawaii. Fern would never have made that mistake. She was a more precise person.

—I can't believe you had sex, Liv said.

—What the fuck do you mean? I thought you were doing it, too. What does it matter?

—It just does. It's just weird. Like, I'm right there. I thought we were just making out with them.

—I don't get why it matters.

—I just think it's kind of, I don't know, low-class.

That was the shit Fern couldn't abide. Liv calling *her* low-class?

Liv regularly got wasted and smeared her lipstick, making coral bridges to her nose, and she embarrassed herself with superiors and told doormen they were handsome young men. Did she want Seb? Who knew? All Fern knew was that she had always been scared of disease and now she wasn't. She didn't care that the Durex broke last night and the ambassador's son fell asleep inside her, dribbling. Contracting HIV would be a godsend.

Her therapist said she was clinically depressed, making it sound like the flu. His name was Sanford; he was wet granola, from Bend, Oregon, with sandy hair and long sideburns. He wore knit ties on top of flannel shirts, like an executive who lived in a tree. My parents died, Fern screamed at him, the third session. Both of them, and we were close. And there is literally nothing left. I'm not depressed. I'm just done. You don't seem to get it; fucking no one does.

And Sanford replied, soulfully, I, too, have lost many people. And proceeded to tell her, for twenty-one minutes on her dime, that he had a meth addict father who left when he was five and a mom who drank tons of boxed white wine and laughed very loudly when any kind of man was around. She smoked Winstons and went out a fair amount, so young Sanford ate a lot of Kraft Macaroni & Cheese; she would make a family-sized package on Sunday, which was the only night she was definitely home, and Sanford would eat it congealed on Mondays, Tuesdays, and Wednesdays, cool and pale orange and flavorless. Toward the weekends it was frozen dinners. Salisbury steak and creamed chipped beef. The latter was his favorite, but he burned himself once opening the steaming plastic and thereafter it was just another thing he loved but was afraid to get close to.

That's not the same thing, Fern had said quietly. To which Sanford countered, How are your bowel movements? She fucking hated it when he asked about bowel movements. Once, he gave her a jar of Friendly Fiber. Yoga and fiber were the keys to a healthy soul.

To Liv she said, Fine, I'm low-class, whatever, man.

—I'm sorry. I didn't mean that. I just think. You're like. Acting out.

—I need to pee.

Liv nudged her chin in the direction of the water and winked.

At half past noon the girls pulled on their cover-ups—a turquoise-and-magenta Roberta Roller Rabbit tunic for Liv, a black velour onesie for Fern—and were seated at the patio for a poolside lunch.

Liv always ordered stupid things. Veal *tonnato* or duck confit over frisée. This day she had the sourdough rabbit sandwich. It smelled like earth and vitamins. Fern ordered the lemon Caesar salad with shards of Parmesan and shimmering anchovy filets.

A conga line of suntanned blond women with tight, tight faces approached their table in succession. Liv's mom's friends. They wanted to talk about what their daughters were doing versus what Liv was doing. Liv was doing stand-up and Upright Citizens Brigade. She had a day job as the executive assistant to the guy who founded Beardz, the app linking gay men with the girls who wanted to go to Barneys and eat lunch with them.

One of the women, Sheila, lingered for nearly five minutes. She had red hair and old-lady freckles and her neck looked two decades older than her face. Her daughter, Jess, had married an "entrepreneur" and they lived all the way out in Vail. Jess was seven months pregnant, but still hiking. Your mom is so lucky, Sheila said, after confirming Liv was single, to have you close to home. Fern marveled at how many dead people were still alive.

While Sheila droned, Fern looked through her phone. No messages, nothing from Seb, or any of the other men she had lately provided with off-the-cuff orgasms. She was still getting used to not having to call her mother in the morning.

When Sheila walked away, Liv hissed, You can't have your phone out at the club!

Fern placed her phone down and stared at her.

—My dad could get written up.

—What a stupid rule.

—You don't have to be here.

—Fine, Fern said, pushing out her rattan chair, scraping the slate floor.

—I'm sorry, Liv said. I think I'm getting my period. Can you sit down?

—Is this about last night?

—What? No.

—Did you like the other one?

—No. I didn't like either of them; I don't care, OK. Look, can you just please try my fucking rabbit sandwich? You'll love it. Pause, smile. It's what the courtesans used to eat.

Fern smiled, too. I can't. Fern was worried about gaining weight. She was thin like a snake, and it meant a lot to her. It felt like she took up less room and so when she went it would be like a thread of angel hair slipping through the hole of a colander.

—Just try it, Liv said, holding out a taupe forkful. You can puke it up after.

Fern ate it; Liv watched her with a big smile. And Fern remembered how it used to be, in the honeymoon of their friendship, after Fern's father died but before her mother was diagnosed. They'd attended nearby high schools but hadn't met until a Thanksgiving Eve party hosted by a mutual friend. They clicked that night; Fern liked how Liv was pounding shots while knitting a blanket. They quickly became close, texting constantly throughout the workday and going out at night, leaving notes for bearded maître d's, sharing tea cakes with Japanese businessmen.

Liv suggested a trip to Capri that summer, where the girls wore linen sundresses and white bikinis and paid thirty euros for muslin sacks and lay out on the black rocks over the Tyrrhenian, shoulder to shoulder. Fern showed Liv the restaurant under the lemon grove where her parents had their first date. Liv insisted on ordering the same dishes they did. The crust on the white pizza gave like the flesh of a child's arm. Liv had never seen fried zucchini flowers. They drank limoncello from cordial glasses and squeezed the sweet-smelling lemons on everything, their fish, their wrists, and a waiter made them garlands of bougainvillea and thyme to wear around their heads.

But their love was cemented the following spring, after the second funeral, when Fern texted Liv, *Come get me?* And Liv showed up within the hour, in her father's cherry-red Aston Martin convertible, blasting LCD Soundsystem, and they drove out to the Colorado Cafe, where they drank everything they could think of and rode the mechanical bull and pulsed onstage with the Kenny Rogers cover band, and wound up in some New Jersey cowboy's apartment, taking turns puking in the bathroom while the cowboy tried to finger whoever was waiting her turn on the couch.

In the morning, when they drove home and Fern said at least nobody was worried about her, Liv brought her back to her house, where Liv's mom raged at them both.

So Fern knew it was important to let Liv know the plan.

—Did I ever tell you how I was obsessed with Jeremy Mullen when I was twelve, you know, from that stupid movie at the aquarium?

—The child actor who hung himself.

—When I found out he killed himself, I was like fuck. I thought, If only he knew how I loved him. I would have taken care of him. You know? I would have done his laundry or told the maid what was dry-clean only.

—Yeah, said Liv, sounding exhausted.

—Now I'm like, fuck no. Whatever ridiculous child actor nonsense. I would have just stolen his pills.

—Probably he had a small dick. That's why he killed himself.

—My point is, it doesn't matter. He killed himself because it was time. Every night is the same, going to clubs, whatever; it doesn't fix anything.

—I think if we were celebrities going to the Chateau every night, we'd make it work, you and me. Anyway, I totally disagree with you. I think people can be saved by people who love them. You just have to be dedicated. You have to like, be there, every day.

—I couldn't save my mom.

—Your parents died of fucking *can*cer, man.

—My mom's was basically suicide. Suicide by cancer.

Liv snorted. But covered Fern's hand with her own. Liv's nails were bitten, but she had pretty, feminine fingers. Fern's hands were small, boyish. They looked silly giving hand jobs.

—What did your mom call your dad again? Liv said.

Liv was obsessed with Fern's dead parents. Because the girls had only become very close in the last several years, Liv hadn't known Fern's parents very well, but she'd made it a mission to understand who they were, how they would answer a certain question. She often made Fern tell her the romantic story of how they met in the Conad, next to the *piadina* display. And in general would say things like, I bet your mom would tell you that you look like a slut right now.

—Pip, Fern said, removing her hand from under Liv's.

Liv smiled and nodded. Pip, she repeated. Then she sat up straight in her chair. Oh my god, see that guy?

—Which?

—Hot dad, twelve o'clock, curly salt-and-pepper hair. And the wife, that polar blonde, and their two little girls, oh my god I'm obsessed. Look at those curly ringlets! They are the perfect family. He's the CFO of the USGA. They live on Flat Pond Road, that sick house with the fucking turrets.

—Awesome.

—That's what I want. He's in the city all week, killing it; she's lounging at the pool with her kids; he comes home on the weekend, they have hot sex and then whatever, she goes to the movies, makes cashew milk. That could be you and me. With powerful husbands, I mean.

—Dude, he probably cheats on her all week. Where Liv liked to imagine perfect marriages because they made her feel she would someday have one, too, Fern liked to expose the rot at the bottom of the bowl of organic vegetables. She looked at the man, tall and patrician in Vilebrequin shorts and fine leather sandals. The wife, with a former-model look, in a white linen shirt over a black bikini.

—No way, Liv said. Look at her.

—She looks like a cleaner, less bloated version of you. Who cares? All women get cheated on.

—You're full of poisonous energy. I'm gonna need to do a juice cleanse when I get home.

—Yeah, vodka's a great base for a cleanse. Listen. Do you want to come back to my house with me? I have to pick up the surrogate certificate for the lawyer. Fern didn't like showing up to the house alone unless she was blasted. And she knew Liv never wanted the day to end.

—Of course. Let's just say hi.

Liv introduced Fern to the man. His name was Chip. He didn't look like a Chip. He looked like a Luther. His lips were fleshy and his skin was moist. The wife looked bored, but she asked after Liv's mom. Chip said he wanted to play with Liv's dad in the Labor Day scramble. But the whole time Chip was looking at Fern and Fern was looking back. Even when another tan man in tennis whites walked past and clapped Chip on the shoulder, saying, Drink later? Chip nodded, said, Always, but kept his shark eyes on Fern.

Fern's house was a museum of mid-century nothing special. Things that were semi-expensive but mismatched, and dowry items from Fiesole. Persian rugs and parquet floors. Silver tea sets on baroque tables. Her parents had kept two entire rooms in the house unused. The couches had just barely escaped those giant plastic condoms. Like her mother before her, Fern never opened the windows or drew the shades. Skeins of sunlight slithered through moth holes in the curtains, and died inside the cracks of the parquet.

Liv was reverential in the house, gliding around like Fern's parents were merely asleep.

Fern couldn't wait to get rid of everything, all the knickknacks. She was going to sell the junk at one of those estate sales usually reserved for the dusty passing of grandparents. A lady named Tabitha would come and man a cash register. Women with skeletal noses would haggle over the price of costume jewelry and oven mitts.

—Your mom had such regal taste, Liv said, her hand resting on a yellow silk scarf with a fringe of tinkling gold leaves.

—You want that? You can have it.

—No, don't be silly.

—Seriously, take it. Or somebody's grandmother will be wearing it to chemo next week.

—Okay, thanks. Liv wrapped it around her neck. She disappeared upstairs, where she spritzed herself with Fern's mom's L'Air du Temps and returned with her nose scrunched up.

—It smells kinda bad in the upstairs bathroom.

—Why'd you go in there? I said don't go in there.

—Sorry, I forgot. Are these them? Liv's hand hovered by the bowl of candies on the kitchen table.

—Yeah.

—Wow. They're pretty cool looking. Where do you get them?

—Some cousin sent those from Italy, but I heard some store in Cranford sells them now. My mom would have been psyched. Or maybe she wouldn't have been. Nothing made that bitch happy.

Liv was about to have one. Fern looked at her.

—What?

—Nothing. I was just kind of doing a thing.

—What kind of a thing, weirdo?

—I don't know. When they're all gone, I was thinking of killing myself. For the past few months, every time Fern did something gross, she would eat a candy. The bowl had been dwindling slowly but surely.

—You fucking idiot. That's retarded.

—Pancreatic, metastatic, Fern whisper-sang, like a rap.

—Will you please come to dinner with us? Don't make me do it alone.

Liv had dinner plans with her former prom-queen sister in the city that night. They would eat somewhere that served peppery Pinot Noir in Ball jars and Liv's sister would talk about her latest private equity douchebag and tell Liv she might land a boyfriend if she lost fifteen pounds.

—Nah, Fern said.

—Dude, you can't stay in your dead mom and dead dad's house. Come back to the city with me. Or I can stay? I'll cancel on the hyena.

—No.

—Ew, you have a suburban dick appointment. A fucking dentist with a wet bar.

—No, man. I just want to like, sit in the house, go through stuff before the house sale. I'm fine. Just leave me alone. Often, Fern made the pain of her parents' loss bigger to get out of doing things she didn't want to do. Other times, she felt it more acutely than it was possible to explain.

—It's weird you have no soul, when your parents had all this love for each other, and for you. Liv scratched at Fern's chest like a chipmunk. Where's your thump thump, Baby Jane?

Fern pushed her away.

—Dude. Stop.

———

After Liv left and just before sunset, Fern put on her mother's snake dress. It was a short-sleeved beige shift with a cream-and-gray viper that twisted around the body. She selected the fawn Trussardi bag from her mother's good-bag shelf and slipped in her license and sixty dollars in cash.

She drove her father's aquamarine Chevy Cavalier to Martini. She played no music. The sky was peach, hot orange, and lilac. She passed sated lawns, cobblestone drives, Maremma sheepdogs. Fast walkers with bony butts in a rainbow of Lululemon black.

Martini was the town bar and it was full of big-bellied insurance lawyers, divorcés in open-toed boots.

Fern sat down and ordered a Blue Hawaii.

Across the bar she saw the man from the country club. His greasy tendrils of black-and-silver hair looked alive. He wore a shirt with a contrast collar and was surrounded by middle-aged men with shiny lips and no wives.

Fern sipped her drink. She could be mostly normal in the day and then the second it got dark her skin and scalp would itch and she'd grow dizzy and exhausted. Next, a sting behind her heart, where the pancreas was, and her lungs would feel heavy and soft with water, like her mother's. (It's like your mother's lungs are drowning, the hipster resident had said, that final week.) Hypochondria, Fern's therapist said a month later, nodding, jotting it down with his Yellowstone Park twig pencil.

She'd got her period that afternoon, so at least she wouldn't be pregnant with the ambassador's son's baby. That would suck, being pregnant. Would she get the abortion and *then* exterminate herself? Or just kill two birds with one bottle of Ambien. Bam.

She'd met a guy here a few years back, just after her dad died and before she met Liv. His name was Teddy. He had a new beagle puppy at home and asked if Fern wanted to meet him. He was one of those rich kids with no focus. A few lame producer credits, several gaudy friends in the fashion world. His fingers became a butterfly inside her, nice, but otherwise she drove home at four a.m., feeling like garbage. Her mother was waiting in the foyer—smoking, gaunt, medieval. How dare you? she said. How dare you to make me worry?

This night Fern didn't feel pretty; she'd used up all her pretty the previous night. But it didn't matter in New Jersey. In New Jersey you just had to be under forty, under 130 pounds, and your hair shoulder length or longer. Preferably straight and dark. That was really it.

Chip sauntered over. Frank Sinatra was pining from the speakers.

—You're Bob Long's daughter's friend; we met today.

—Oh, right.

—Is . . . uh-hmm here?

—Liv? No. She went back to the city.

—Must be nice to be young and living in the city.

—The time of our lives.

—You here by yourself?

—Yup.

—Can I buy you a drink? You wanna come hang with a couple of old fogeys?

He sniffed. Clearly he had cocaine.

Fern sniffed, winked. He smiled. He got close and moved a tiny vial into her palms. He pressed it down with the pork of his thumb. When you're done, he said, meet us on the patio for a Cuban.

In the faux-elegant bathroom, Fern saw the makeup on her face was like a mask. It looked like it could be peeled off to reveal a dead person.

She snorted two lines off the tank of the toilet with a one-dollar bill. She rubbed some on her gums. She wondered if her parents were watching.

The patio was full of white wizard smoke blown from the mouths of the horniest men she had ever seen. Chip was hitting on one of the waitresses who drove in every day from Linden. Fern pretended she hadn't seen him and began to walk back inside. She felt a hand on her shoulder, and smelled his clean laundry.

—You almost missed us, he said.

She ordered a Glenfiddich on his tab. She asked the waitress for honey and poured some into her glass, saying this was what they did in Scotland.

—Is that a fact? said the fattest man.

—Yeah. Plus it takes the sting off the liquor, for the baby.

—Say what? You're pregnant?

—Yup, Fern said, rubbing her belly. I'm drinking for two.

—She's joking, said Chip, smiling.

—She's funny. Hey, you're funny.

—Beautiful babies, said another man. You know that? You're beautiful babies. He was looking from Fern to the waitress and back, as though they knew each other. The waitress had chunky highlights and a pierced eyebrow.

One of the other guys, who looked like he'd had a face lift, bought a whole bottle of Patrón. Fern did shots with them. Chip held the lime wedge as she sucked it.

Face Lift said, Snapper these days, drink like men.

Chip asked her what her father did. Actually, he said, Who's your father? But it was the same question.

—Nobody, Fern said. She thought how her father had never gone to a bar with the guys in all the years she'd known him.

She heard the fattest man say, Daddy issues, under his breath. She swayed and Chip caught her. She whispered something into his ear.

—You wanna go where? he said.

She said it again.

He raised his eyebrows and smiled. I know just the place.

They passed the florist with the mirrored door and she checked her body in the mirror. Her mother's best dress, her tan legs. They got into Chip's olive Jaguar. He was drunk, too. Fern was impressed that certain men always knew how to drive, to move through tollbooths without scraping the sides, even when they were three martinis deep. At home the Ambien was in the medicine closet with the cancer accoutrements—steroids, laxatives, vibrant head scarves. Fern felt like she was in a sensory deprivation tank. She thought of Liv's sunny face and wished she were with her now, her warm, solid arms around Fern.

They pulled up to a cement building, seemingly windowless. A pink scripted sign said, CHEEQUES.

Had she suggested this? She didn't remember. Probably she did.

Inside a guy wearing a Method Man shirt gave them a spot in the front row. Red velvet banquettes, glass tables, purple lighting. Chip ordered kamikaze shots and Scotch and beer.

Most of the dancers were younger than Fern. One dark-skinned girl was absolutely beautiful; she could have been working in Abercrombie and dating someone with a good family.

There weren't many people in there, so the stripper concentrated on them, specifically on Fern; she whooshed her long mane in Fern's face. Fern inhaled. Salon Selectives conditioner, she was positive, probably from a dollar store, left over from 1994. It was her mother's brand. Crème rinse, the old lady called it.

Not to be outdone, Fern stood and did a dance for Chip. She ripped the seams of her mother's dress, straddling his lap. She licked the outlines of his giant lips with her tongue. The look on his face was not shock, or even happy surprise. It was almost judgmental. She just wanted to feel sexier than the stripper.

He drove her back to her car, parked in the unlit lot outside Maximilian Furs and the out-of-business toy store. It was past three in suburbia and there was no one on the streets. He turned to look at her; then they were kissing again; his tongue was cold and his mouth tasted like iceberg lettuce. Eventually he got his manicured hands up her mother's dress. She remembered her tampon, yanked it out, opened the door, and tossed it in the street. What they did after that didn't register. All Fern could think was that she would be eating two candies when she got home.

Last month over Sazeracs at Buvette, Liv said, When I get married I'm going to have to watch my husband around you. You, and your shifty labia. Liv said that because she'd just met Teddy—of the beagle and the butterfly fingers—through her parents, and told Fern about him, and Fern said, Oh, I effed that loser. Liv ended up going on two dates with Teddy. She didn't like him, but she slept with him. Did you enjoy my sloppy seconds? Fern said. Why are you a dick? Liv said. What does it do for you? Later that night, they really got into it. They'd moved on to a dim Mexican speakeasy on the Lower East Side. Liv was blasted on tequila. The fight erupted at the bar, quiet and nasty, their eyes locked on each other. Fern threw down a fifty-dollar bill—she was flush with cash these days—and walked fast down Ludlow. Liv threw open the door of the place and came after her, plastering Fern's little body against a parked SUV. She held Fern's neck against a cool window with her big hands. What are you so proud of? Liv said, nearly spitting in Fern's face. You're jealous of me, Fern said, smirking. You're a cunt, Liv said. A fucking loveless whore. They wrestled in each other's arms, pushing, pinching skin between gel nails, pulling hair. In the end, Fern had a split lip and in the morning Liv touched her middle finger to her mouth, then inspected her finger for blood, mimicking Fern the night before.

Now Fern drove home from Martini, falling asleep several times at the wheel and waking only when her car slid into the dirt off the shoulder. When she saw the bricks of her dark house, she was shocked she'd made it back alive.

She crept in as though her parents would hear her if she made noise. In the upstairs bathroom she vomited in the sink and not the toilet, because the toilet contained some precious urine—her mother's final home pee, lime colored now and smelling like science. She lay in her parents' bed, a king made out of two twin mattresses. But vomiting had diluted forty percent of the drunk, while the coke was still blooming, and now she couldn't sleep.

She thought of the bowl of candies, and said out loud, Three. This night deserved three.

Quietly she slunk down the stairs. She passed the antique mirror on the wall, which as a child she thought could reflect the demons in her soul. Now it said twenty-five dollars or best offer.

It was bizarre, to be in the house without the snores of the dog and the fear of the parents. So weird how a whole house of people could disappear over the course of three Fall Previews.

She wasn't exactly shocked, but her jaw did kind of drop when she saw the bowl of candies utterly replenished. She imagined Liv, driving out to the importer in Cranford, coming back, and letting herself in the screen door at the back, a burglar in a beach cover-up. Filling the bowl, *lacrime d'amore* tinkling the glass.

Fern admired them. Pale shells, delicate as the eyelids of newborns.

Here were hundreds more shitty things she could do to herself. On South Orange Avenue an ambulance *awayoed*, followed by the silence of the upper-middle dead.

She sat down and started popping the candies in her mouth, one after another. Beautiful babies, she thought, laughing, all of us.

CREDITS

"Ghost Lover" — published in *McSweeney's*

"Forty-Two" — published in *New England Review*

"Beautiful People" — published in the *Sewanee Review*

"Padua, 1966" — published in *Harper's*

"Grace Magorian" — published in *Esquire*

"Maid Marian" — published in *Granta*

"A Suburban Weekend" — published in *Granta*

ABOUT THE AUTHOR

Lisa Taddeo is the author of the #1 *New York Times* bestseller *Three Women*, which she is adapting as a dramatic series at Showtime, and the novel *Animal*. She has contributed to the *New York Times*, *New York*, *Esquire*, *Elle*, *Glamour*, and many other publications. Her nonfiction has been included in the *Best American Sports Writing* and *Best American Political Writing* anthologies, and her short stories have won two Pushcart Prizes. She lives with her husband and daughter in New England.